"I want you to accept a favor," said the Mexican.

"Humph!" grunted Lascar. "Well?"

"You hate one man a good deal."

"Do I?"

"The Montana Kid, no?"

Jack Lascar glanced over his shoulder at the door. He looked at the window, also. Then he finished the white fire of his tequila and stared at Rubriz.

"Damn him!" Lascar hissed. "I will send him to hell one day!"

The Mexican smiled. "I can bring him to you."

MAX BRAND

WRITING AS EVAN EVANS

MONTANA RIDES AGAIN

CHARTER
NEW YORK

A DIVISION OF CHARTER COMMUNICATIONS INC.
A GROSSET & DUNLAP COMPANY
51 Madison Avenue
New York, New York 10010

MONTANA RIDES AGAIN

Copyright © 1935 by Frederick Faust

An Ace Charter Book

First Ace Charter printing: January 1982

Published simultaneously in Canada

2 4 6 8 0 9 7 5 3 1
Manufactured in the United States of America

MONTANA RIDES AGAIN

CHAPTER I

THE strides of Brother Pascual were long and swift, but
the day strode longer and swifter by far to its ending.
Shadows as blue as water were flowing through the
ravines, rising higher and higher, and the naked summits
of the San Carlos range began to burn with rose and
with golden flame against that Mexican sky; but the
friar, taking a stronger hold on the staff which was his
companion in the wilderness, gave little heed to the
beauty around him. He had only one eye for it, after
all; over the other he wore a big shield of black leather.
A plaster patch made a big white cross on the opposite
cheek and a bandage circled his head. To give his stride
greater freedom he had pulled up his long grey robe so
that a fold hung over the cord that girdled him and the
edge of his garment kicked in and out around his knees.
In the calf of each brown and hairy leg there was a
mighty fist of muscle needed for the support of this
towering bulk of a man, yet the only provision he
carried with him on his journey was a pouch of dry
corn meal. He was dark as an Indian, but his broad face
was marked with the pain and the doubt of some high
endeavour.

The sun bulged its cheeks in the west and blew
radiant colour all across the sky; the heavens darkened
to green and amber, then yellow-green and blue, with

the green fading rapidly into night as Brother Pascual came to the narrow mouth of a gorge over which leaned pillars of lofty rock. A jack rabbit darted from behind a stone and fled, leaving the whisper of its speed in the air. And in the mouth of the ravine the friar paused and shouted:

"Oh-ho! Oh-ho! I am Brother Pascual! Hai! Do you hear! I am Brother Pascual!"

After a moment, while the echoes were still dimly flying, a voice almost at his elbow said:

"Well, brother, who's hungry now? Whose belly-ache are you to tell us about now?"

"Is it Luis?" asked the friar.

"Luis went spying once too often into the stock-yards at Chihuahua. They killed him in the slaughter-house. Maybe they made him into sausage. Damned stringy sausage he must have made, too!"

"What is your name? Ah, you are Carlos!"

"You've only seen me once; and it's too dark for seeing now, unless you're a cat. How do you remember people, Brother?"

"I remember them by their need of mercy," said the friar. "Poor Luis! Is he gone? He had a need of mercy, also."

"So has every man with Rubriz," answered Carlos.

"So have I. So have all mortals," declared Brother Pascual, humbly. "I am going on to the house."

"There's plenty of noise in the house," said Carlos. "Yesterday we caught a mule train loaded with——"

"I don't want to hear it," broke in Pascual. "We are all sinners, Carlos. But good may come out of evil. Good may come out of evil. Saint Nicholas, be large in the eye of my mind!"

With that, he stalked on through the thick blackness of the ravine, which rapidly widened. Trees choked the way. With his long staff he fended his course through them until he came out on a level valley floor, with a stippling of lights nearby giving a vague outline of a house.

He heard singing and shouting and the beat of running feet while he was still in the distance, and, though he was one pledged to love good and hate evil, he could not help smiling a little. For Pascual was in many respects a true peon and therefore he had to forgive a true *bandido* like Mateo Rubriz. A thief steals from all alike; a *bandido* harries the rich only; and in Mexico there is a belief that grows out of the very soil that all rich men are evil.

When he came to the door of the house he beat on it three times with his staff. Then he threw the door open on the smoky light of the inner hall, and shouted:

"I, Brother Pascual, am coming! It is I, Brother Pascual!"

The thunder of his voice rumbled through the house, and then a door flung open to his right and let a rush of sound flow out about him.

"Bring in Pascual!" shouted the familiar, strident tones of Mateo Rubriz.

Half a dozen wild young fellows leaped through the doorway and seized on the burly friar and drew him into the room. It was the kitchen, dining-hall and reception-chamber of Mateo Rubriz. As a chorus of welcome rose to greet Brother Pascual, he snuffed up at the fragrance of roasting kid—most delicious of all meat in this world; and the savour of frijoles cooked with peppers, and the pungency of coffee, and the thin scent of beer and the sour of wine—all were in that air.

At the long table some of the men were still eating; others looked on with a careless interest as Mateo Rubriz, equipped with a small balance-scale, measured out lumps of shining white metal and small heaps of heavy yellow dust.

Brother Pascual refused to call it silver and gold because money is the root of all evil, and he loved these men in spite of himself. So he fastened his gaze only on the huge squat figure of Mateo Rubriz, who wore common cotton trousers, furled up to his knees, and cheap huaraches on his feet. The sleeves of his shirt were cut off near the armpit so as to leave unhampered that vast strength, which, men said, was unrivalled in all the San Carlos range, in all Mexico, perhaps, and therefore in the world!

So thought Pascual. And he rejoiced in the might of that fellow peon in his ragged, dirty clothes; he rejoiced in the red silk cap that Rubriz preferred to all the sombreros of cloth or of straw. And the heart of Pascual was touched with sympathy when he marked, diagonally across the flushed face of Mateo, the long white scar which the whiplash had left on the flesh. Men said that no single whip-stroke could have left such a broad and deep scar, but that Mateo Rubriz, in the passion of his shame and hate, had rubbed salt into his wound to freshen it and keep it burning on his face as rage burned in his heart. At any rate, there was the sign clearly visible whenever his face reddened—which was often.

"Come here, little old Pascual!" Rubriz was thundering. "What have you been doing to yourself? I've told you that if you keep taking your short cuts through the mountains, up the cliffs and down the Devil's Slides, you'd have a fall one of these days. Well, if you've had a fall like that, thank God that your head was battered but not broken. Come here and dip your hands into that sack—all gold—and take out the fill of your big hands. You can weight down your pockets and spend it all on your poor. You can buy a new mule for your *arriero*, a new cow for your housewife, and a new gun for the hunter, a new trap for the trapper. You can give sheep to the shepherd and cattle to the poor *charro*. Dip in your hands as deep as the wrists and pull out what your fingers will hold. Come, Pascual! Hai, my children! We shall all be a thousand leagues nearer to heaven when Brother Pascual has prayed for us."

Brother Pascual stood by the bandit and looked down at the buckskin sack which held such treasure. He was aware, too, of the gleam of white metal and of yellow up and down the table. He took a deep breath and looked up to the smoke-blackened rafters of the room.

"Father, forgive them!" he said from his heart. Then he added: "Not even for my poor, Mateo. Give me something to eat, as soon as I have washed. But stolen money poisons even the poor."

Mateo caught him by the wrists and looked him up and down, half savage and half fond.

"Listen to me! Be silent, everyone. Mateo Rubriz is speaking. Do you hear? One day I shall give up this life and go into a desert with this good man. I shall scratch up roots with my bare hands and feed on them. I shall drink nothing but clear spring water—give me a cup of that wine, one of you!—and I shall spend the rest of my days praying and doing penance."

He seized a great jewelled cup which was handed to him, brimming with sour red wine, and poured half the contents down his throat.

"When I do penance," he roared, "it shall be the greatest penance that ever was done by a Mexican, and Mexicans are the only men."

He made a gesture, and some of the wine slopped out of the cup and splashed from the floor on to the bare hairy calves of his legs.

9

"Do you hear me, Pascual? By God! I shall be such a saint, one day, that they'll have to shift in their chairs and crowd their haloes closer together to make room for Mateo Rubriz. Give me some more wine, some one. I have not tasted a drink for a month of desert days. Pascual, go wash, if you please, and then come back and eat. San Juan of Capistrano! there is redder blood in me than this wine, and every drop of it sings when I see such a good man."

Brother Pascual went to the well outside the room, in the little patio, and there, as he threw off his long robe and washed the sweat and the sand of the travel from his body, he could hear the voice of Rubriz, still, exclaiming:

"The rest of you—all swine at a trough. There is no other man in the world. There is only Brother Pascual!"

When Pascual came back into the room, he found a huge platter of kid hot from the turning of the spit and a mass of frijoles and thin, limber, damp tortillas. He used the tortillas as spoon and fork. A knife from his wallet was his carver.

As he ate, he sipped moderately from a big glass of the red wine. Pulque, as a matter of fact, would have been more to his truly Mexican taste. The division of the spoils had been completed and the treasure was cleared from the table, though still a bright yellow dust appeared here and there on the rough wood. The wages of ten labourers for a month were wasted out of the superfluity of these robbers. Mateo Rubriz himself was now eating again, walking up and down with his jewelled wine cup in one hand and in the other a fat joint from which he tore long shreds with those powerful teeth of his.

"Now is the time to speak, Lucio," said Rubriz.

"You have been sitting there with fire in your eyes, devouring José with glances. Tell me what was wrong."

Lucio stood up. He lacked the rounded, blubbery face of a peon; his features were more the type of the aristocrat and his cheeks were so hollow that they pulled at the corners of his mouth and kept him with the semblance of a sneering smile. He said:

"José, stand up!"

"Ay, to you or to any man!" said a youth with very wide shoulders and very bowed legs. He was the true peon type. He swaggered out and stood well forward on the floor.

"When they came chasing after us," said Lucio, "my horse went down under me. I ran as well as my legs would carry me. I heard hoof-beats. I looked back and saw that a friend was riding up. It was José. I held out my hand to let him help me up, but, by St. Christopher! he galloped right past me! He even tried to look the other way. And the Rurales and the soldiers were sure to get me, except that I found a crack among the rocks and ran and fell into it like a lizard. Mateo Rubriz, give me a judgment! Is that fellowship? A lame dog would be better treated by its fellows!"

A little murmur came out of the throats of the crowd. It was not loud, but it was high-pitched, and therefore the friar knew the strain of anger from which it proceeded.

"Now speak, José," said Rubriz.

"This!" said José, loudly. "I saw Lucio running, of course. I wanted to help him. But I had a whole sack of the gold in the saddle bag. To throw away myself and my horse—that was nothing, though the Rurales were sure to catch us both if I tried to make the pinto carry double. But there was the gold. So I rode on.

Speak up with a big voice, Lucio. Are you worth thirty pounds of gold?"

Lucio said nothing. He looked ready to leap at José, but he could not bring up words from his throat.

The whole room was hushed. Men leaned from their places, their eyes intent on the leader, who still walked calmly up and down. But now he paused and pointed the ragged joint of roast meat at José.

"Silver is a good thing and gold is better, but silver and gold and emeralds and diamonds are not worth one drop of blood. Blood is better than money. José, you have not been with me long. You have not learned. Otherwise, by San Juan of Capistrano! I would hang you from that rafter with my own hands! Ride by a dismounted comrade? Leave a friend behind for the Rurales? However, you have been with me only a short time. What I tell you now you will remember. No?"

"I will remember," said José, suddenly abashed and staring at the floor.

"Are you satisfied, Lucio?" asked the master.

"No," said Lucio.

"Take knives, then. Strip to the waist. Carve each other or kill each other. That is the law. But we'll have no hatreds inside my band of *charros*."

"Good!" said José, and began to tear off his jacket.

Lucio said nothing, but there was speech in the burning of his eyes and in his sneering lips.

That was when Brother Pascual stood up and went to Lucio.

"Lucio," he said, "when your brother was sick in the mountains, I searched till I found him and carried him into the camp on my shoulders."

"Therefore," said Lucio, "ask me for my right hand and it is yours."

"Give it to me, then," said the gigantic friar. So he

took the right hand of the astonished Lucio and half led and half dragged him across the floor to confront José. "Give your hand to me, José," he commanded.

"My hand is my own," said José, sullenly.

The huge grip of Pascual closed suddenly on the nape of José's neck. He shook the young bandit violently. A knife flashed into the hand of José. It jerked back, but it was not driven home into the great, fearless breast of Brother Pascual. It was awe of the friar rather than the fierce yell that went up from the others that caused the knife to drop to the floor.

"Now give me your hand!" shouted Pascual, enraged, "or I'll carry you out and throw you into the slime of the hog-wallow, where I've thrown bigger and stronger men than you!"

"Brother, forgive me!" said José, helplessly, and he gave his right hand. Pascual instantly clapped it into that of Lucio. He stood over the two men, who glared at one another.

"José is a fool, but he is a young fool and he can learn wisdom," boomed Pascual. "Lucio, grip his hand. I, Brother Pascual, command you. José, tell him that you were wrong. A sulky man is worse than a sulky dog. But a confession washes the heart clean."

There was a moment of pause, so tense that the breathing of the men in the room could be heard, and the ripping sounds as Mateo Rubriz tore at his joint of roast meat.

Then José said, suddenly, weakly:

"I was wrong. Lucio, I hated you because you got the black mare that I wanted. Will you forget?"

"Is it true?" said Lucio, stunned and gaping. "Do you confess this before them all? Then you are my brother!" And suddenly he had flung his arms around José.

"I am shamed—but I was wrong," said José.

"Shamed?" cried Lucio. "I kill the man who smiles!"

But there was no smiling. Only Mateo Rubriz hurled towards the hearth the big bone which he had picked clean. It clanged loudly against an iron pot and spun into the ashes, knocking up a white cloud.

"By the blood of God!" cried Rubriz, "my men have turned into women. Well, let them go so long as I have you, Pascual. Have you only come here to make my poor fellows drop their knives on the floor?"

"I have come to speak seriously with you, Mateo," answered the big friar.

"You hear that he wants to speak to me!" called Rubriz to the rest. "Then why do you wait? You have money in your wallets and food in your bellies. Go, drink yourselves to sleep and be damned. Away with you!"

CHAPTER II

THEY faced one another across the long table.

"Tell me about your tumble, first," suggested Rubriz. "Well, even the mountain sheep break their necks now and again. If something hit you near the eye, thank your God that you are not blinded."

"The gun butt hit the bone over my eye; that was all," said the friar.

"Gun butt?" said Rubriz, suddenly scowling. Then he pointed. "Gun butt, eh? And what hit the other side of your face?"

"The point of a knife," answered Brother Pascual. "But it was nothing."

The bandit began to steal around the table as though he hoped to surprise news in the very mind of his big friend.

"And your head? The bandage, there?" he demanded.

"That is not very bad, either. The bullet glanced; I have a hard skull——"

"The butt of a gun—a knife—a bullet. Splendour of God! what fools have forgotten that you are the friend of Mateo Rubriz?"

"The governor of Duraya and his soldiers."

"General Ignacio Estrada? Where did he dare to beat you?"

"In the Church of Our Lady of Guadalupe."

"The governor—beats you—in the church! Am I going mad? What were you doing?"

"Fighting a little, Mateo, to keep the governor and the rest of the masked men from stealing the emerald crown of Our Lady."

"Why, brother, that crown was stolen long years ago!"

"It was found again by a peon whose son was very sick. He brought the crown back to the church; his son was healed; and then the governor stole the emeralds and the gold again."

"How was he known, if his face was masked?"

"The holy bishop recognized the voice of the principal robber."

"Bishop Emiliano?"

"Yes."

"Ah," cried Rubriz, "that little man may be as thin as a knife, but he can cut as deep. He knows me, does he not?"

"You have made many good presents to the church."

"It knows my gold and it knows my silver. Do you hear, brother? When the name of Rubriz is spoken in that church, all the shadows stir and the statues whisper a prayer for me. I tell you this: in that church alone I have bought half the distance from hell to heaven."

The friar smiled a little.

"But this Estrada—what do you tell me about him? No good man ever wore the name of general—except Bonita Juarez—except Bonita Juarez—God rest his soul!"

"God rest his soul!" echoed the friar, devoutly. "But General Estrada came into the church. The poor monks ran away. Only the bishop guarded the image of Our Lady——"

"I would rather have one blessing from him than ten thousand Aves from a whole college of singing priests——"

"Peace, Mateo!" commanded the friar, sternly.

He went on:

"The holy bishop recognized the voice of the general and called out his name; and Estrada desired to leave no witness behind him. He struck Bishop Emiliano to the floor."

"That poor bald head! Did it crack like an egg shell?" asked Rubriz.

"Our Lady had softened the blow or made it glance. The bishop lives, and the governor sits in his fort with the crown of Our Lady and the ten emeralds in it."

"But you were there yourself?" demanded Rubriz, his face swelling and purpling with emotion.

"It had taken me a little time to get to my knees because I had been very deep in a prayer. I came shouting at them. But they struck down the holy bishop. I took a pair of the soldiers and knocked their heads together."

"San Juan of Capistrano! If only I had been there to see and to help!"

"The two soldiers fell down. I knocked over another, but I tripped on him, and he stabbed at me and put the point of his knife in my cheek. As I was getting up a gun exploded; I felt that blow on my head as the bullet struck; and another man hit me over the eye with the butt of a gun. I tried to keep my wits, but they flew away into darkness like a flock of crows, and I fell on my face."

"May they rot with a blight! I'll put them on their faces! If I don't cut off their eyelids and stake them out in the sun, my name is not——"

"Mateo, be still. The bishop called for me the next day—this morning. He said to me: 'If I complain of the stealing, then all the hawks will gather; the jewels will be scattered through the land. It is better to carry word about this to Mateo Rubriz, because he will not allow this thing to be.'"

"Did he say that?" exclaimed Rubriz, leaping to his feet. "No wonder he's a bishop. If he knows men as well as this, he must know a good bit about saints and angels, also. I shall show him, Pascual, that I am a man to trust. But what does he want me to do? I shall go to Duraya and cut the throat of the general the first time he leaves the fort at night!"

"That would leave the emerald crown still safely inside the fort, Mateo."

"Hai! That is true! But, Pascual, in the name of God the bishop doesn't think that I can fly like a bird or dig like a mole to get into the fort and then stand invisible inside it till I've found the emeralds and taken them? Does he think that?"

The friar sighed. He looked down at his own great hands and was silent.

"But that *is* what he wishes!" muttered Rubriz. He turned pale. On the hair of his bare arm he smeared some of the sweat off his face. "No single man in this world could do the thing!" he cried. "Look at me, Pascual, and tell me that I am right!"

But Pascual, in a misery, continued to stare silently down at his hands, which were gripped hard together.

"I shall find ten other emeralds and make them into a golden crown twice as big," exclaimed Rubriz.

"Mateo, beware of blasphemy!" said the friar.

"True!" groaned Rubriz. "It is a holy thing. It has come from the brow of Our Lady. May God pour the fire of hell into the bones of Estrada! But what can I do—alone?"

"You have many men," said Brother Pascual, softly, as though he wished that his words might become part of the other man's thought.

"I have men? I have hands and feet and guns to help me. But for such work numbers are a loss, not an advantage. To be secret as a snake, quick as a cat's paw, without fear under heaven—all of these things I am—but where is there another to be my brother in the danger? Oh, Pascual, two men together may outface the devil; but one man alone—in the fort of Duraya——"

He threw up his arms with a groan.

"Is there no other man?" asked the friar.

"There is one other, but he could not come."

"Could money buy him?"

"He is rich."

"For the sake of Our Lady?"

"He is a gringo dog," cried Rubriz, pacing the floor, "and Our Lady means nothing to him. Besides, if he were to try to ride south into Mexico, a whisper of his coming would go before him, the stones would yell out under his feet, 'El Keed!' That is how he is hated and wanted by the Rurales, by the soldiers!"

"Ah, Mateo, is this gringo the only man? This man you hate?"

"Ay, this man I hate is the only one. But also I love him, and he loves me. Hai, Pascual! Think that I had him under the muzzle of my gun. That his life was like this, in my hand to crush. And there lay Tonio, the traitor—Pascual, keep me from speaking about it. O God! these are not tears of water that run out of my eyes. They are tears of blood and my heart is weeping. But I let them both go free because Tonio loves me, even while he is wearing another name and speaking another speech. And Montana I saw was the second man in the world. Rubriz, then El Keed. There is no third. I could not kill him. I left the house. I took his hand. We spoke quietly. We were friends. For a little while, as I went away, my heart was so full with my friend that I could forget how I had lost Tonio through him."

Brother Pascual, listening to this speech, was so intent that sweat ran unheeded on his face, faster than the tears of Rubriz. He knew very well that famous tale of how the Montana Kid, by means of a tattooed birthmark, had insinuated himself into the Lavery household in the place of the son whom Rubriz, to repay the whip-stroke, had stolen twenty years before; but then some stroke of conscience had driven the Kid south into Mexico to find the real heir, whom he had seen there in his wanderings.

He knew how Montana had fought to take young "Tonio" away, and how Rubriz, who had raised the boy to love him and hate the "gringos," had resisted desperately and then pursued the pair north towards the Rio Grande. Now Tonio was restored to his blood and his family; he had been sent off to Europe to put some distance between him and his terrible foster father, Rubriz; and the Montana Kid—El Keed in Mexico—remained on the Lavery ranch about to marry the daughter of the family. It was such a story that men were sure to remember it and talk about it. But nothing about it was more strange than that Rubriz respected Montana even more than he hated that reckless young adventurer.

Rubriz blew his nose with a great snoring sound.

"Now I am better," he said.

"This Montana who stole Tonio——" began the friar.

"Be silent!" shouted Rubriz, with the face of a madman.

"If he were with you, might you not steal back the emeralds, even from Fort Duraya and General Estrada? And if you went to El Keed, might he not remember how you once spared him? Might he not ride with you in spite of the danger?"

"He is to marry the sister of Tonio. How can I make him leave her?"

"Mateo, it is not for us to doubt. Let us go north towards the land of the gringos. Let us cross the river. When we have come to the place, God will surely show us the proper way. He will bring even Montana into our hands."

Rubriz, at this, had stopped his pacing. His head began to lift higher and higher.

"Pascual," he said, "who can tell? Perhaps it is true. Perhaps it is the will of God, after all. Perhaps God wishes to see Mateo Rubriz at the side of El Keed. For even God Himself could never guess what two such men might do. It is true! I feel that the thing shall be. We shall ride together; we shall work together; and what will walls of stone be, what will soldiers be, when we two are side by side?"

"But he is a gringo—and ah, the pity of it!" said the friar.

"Ay," groaned Rubriz, "the pity of it! But only his skin is American and his heart is pure Mexican!"

CHAPTER III

In the corral the blood-bay mare was being drawn to the snubbing-post. And that great rider of outlaw horses, Tombstone Joe, was pulling the ropes. The cowpunchers sat like crows on the fence-posts, eight feet from the ground. The Montana Kid was among the crows. From the veranda of the ranch house, he looked like any of the others except that his shoulders were a little wider and the big double cord of back muscle could be distinguished even at that distance, and through the shirt.

Ruth Lavery stood by one of the porch pillars.

"We ought to go down," she said.

"There's no use having too much audience," said Richard Lavery. "That would make Montana want to ride the mare himself."

"He's promised not to," answered the girl. But fear changed the blue of her eyes as she spoke.

"Promises—well, promises are still only words, to Montana," said her father.

"Don't say that," she protested.

"Well, I won't say it, then," answered tall Richard Lavery. But he kept his thought in the grim lines of his face.

"You've never loved him!" said the girl, nervously, still gripping the pillar against which she leaned.

"Honour and respect him I can," said Lavery, curtly. "He's more *man* than anyone I know."

At this she sighed, quickly, as one in whom a great

emotion is constantly pent. And she broke out, suddenly:

"You think he's only a tramp."

"I don't think he's *only* a tramp," said Richard Lavery.

He looked down at a black band around the arm of his coat. His wife had died two months before.

"You think he's a tramp—and something more," said the girl, speaking quietly, mostly to herself. "You sent Dick away to Europe—to get him away from Montana—to get him away from temptation. You've never trusted Montana."

"Now that your mother is gone," said Lavery, very gently, "do you think that he'll be with us long?"

She lifted her head a little. She scanned, as if to find the answer there, the long lines of the valley, and the high plateaux, and the green pasture-lands for miles and miles which all belonged to the Lavery estate. Dick, who was once Tonio Rubriz, would be heir to half of that estate. Montana had brought him back from Mexican oblivion to share the rich heritage. The other half would go to her and to Montana.

"We'll be married Sunday," she said, briefly.

"He's put it off before," said the rancher, and there was no mercy in his hard voice. "He'll put it off again."

"He won't! This is the last time! He knows it." Then she added, in a half-weary, half-sad outburst, "Doesn't he care about me?"

"Ay, he cares about you. And he cares about other things, too. Horses and guns—and his freedom."

Down in the corral, Tombstone Joe walked backwards and looked over the mare. Now that he had snubbed her against the post, other men were blindfolding her, working on bridle and saddle. Ransome, the grey-headed ranch foreman, was in charge of this business.

"What you think of her, Tombstone?" asked Ransome.

"Half dynamite and half wildcat," said Tombstone. "She's too damn pretty to be good."

Said the Montana Kid, from the fence:

"You don't hitch on to a streak of lightning and ask is it good. You ask how far it'll take you."

Tombstone turned sharply around to rebuke the speaker. Then he saw that it was the Kid, and instead of answering he rubbed his jaw, slowly, as though he had been hit there on a day.

The Kid did not smile. His brown, handsome face remained perfectly calm, but as he stared at the mare the blue of his eyes burned paler and brighter continually. He pushed his hat back from his forehead and showed the blue-black of sleeked hair. He was so dark that he looked almost like a Mexican. Only, in moments of excitement the blue of his eyes turned bright and pale. He was like the mare—big, but with sinews and proportions that made him look swift and light.

"This here streak," said Tombstone, "it'll take you far, all right; it'll take you to hell, but it might leave you there."

The Kid tapped the ashes from his cigarette and made no answer. His eyes were on the mare. She was waiting patiently, submitting to the darkness that enveloped her eyes, muffled her thought. And yet there was danger in her patience. Down-headed, still there was nothing about her to suggest the thought of the wild-caught mustang.

In the old days, wild-caught hawks made the best hunting-falcons. She was wild-caught. And she was the best. The Kid knew it. He kept tasting her

24

strength and her speed as he had tasted them since the day when he started with many men on her trail. The length of that trail had caused the third postponement of his marriage with Ruth Lavery. Now he sat on the fence to watch this famous horsebreaker try his hand because Montana had promised, faithfully, never to mount the mare until she was well broken. That was why electric thrills kept starting in his heart and flooding out through his forehead and his finger-tips.

The bridle and the saddle were adjusted. Tombstone mounted gingerly. Many falls had taught him shameless caution. He almost acted like a man afraid.

"Let her go," he said, quietly.

The bandage from her eyes, the rope from her neck, were instantly disengaged. And the mare shot at the sky.

Nobody spoke. They had all seen an infinity of horsebreaking, but this was not the same thing. They stiffened on the fence-posts. They looked with great eyes, seeing and thinking. Horses have to be broken, but the mare looked like Beauty and the man looked like the Beast.

He was a frightened Beast. There was no pretence of the dashing, cavalier ride which a cowpuncher tries to show at a rodeo. Tombstone started that way, sitting straight up, raking the mare fore and aft with his spurs, but after the second jump he was pulling leather like a tenderfoot caught in a horse-storm.

This was a tornado. It rushed as though it would tear down the fence. It turned as though it would bore a hole through the ground. And Tombstone sailed out of the saddle sidewise. He struck the corral soil, raised a dust, struck it again, and lay limp and still.

Three nooses settled over the neck of the mare and held her as she tried to get at the fallen rider and savage him. Someone crawled under the fence and dragged Tombstone to safety. Someone else emptied a canteen over the upturned face of Tombstone. After a while he breathed. Then he stood up.

"She foxed me that time but I'll get her the next try," he said.

Ransome, the foreman, said to the Kid, "Well, what you think?"

"She's a sweetheart," said the Montana Kid.

He eased himself down from the fence. The side of the fence he was on was the inside.

They were snubbing the mare close up to the post again.

Ransome grabbed Montana's arm.

"Look at her," he said. "Don't you be a damn fool. Keep away from temptation."

The Kid looked down at Ransome's hand. Ransome took it away.

"We'll just have a look-see," said the Kid.

"You been and promised Miss Ruth!" said Ransome, huskily.

"Did I?" said the Kid, absently.

He walked around the front of the mare and looked into her eyes. She was quiet. The only thing she had learned was the burn of ropes, and she did not fight. Not outwardly. The devil was quiet in her, waiting.

Someone said, from the fence, "He could handle hell fire, but not *that* fire."

Another man said: "What's her name? What you gunna call her, Montana?"

"You better call her before you're dead," said another.

"Her name's Sally," said the Kid, gently.

He smiled beautifully at the men on the fence. He included them all in the gentleness of his glance. They feared him so much that they almost hated him; but because they loved him, also, no man smiled back.

"Why call her Sally?" asked Ransome, the foreman.

"I knew a gal called Sally once," said the Kid.

"Did she look like this mare?" asked Ransome.

"She wore black silk stockings all around, like this one," said the Kid, gently.

Tombstone Joe was fitting himself carefully into the saddle. Montana said:

"Watch her, Joe."

"Who the hell is giving me advice?" said Tombstone.

Montana sighed and closed his eyes; when he opened them the hoofs of the mare were beating the corral like a drum. The dust went up as thick as water before it explodes into spray. Through the rifts, or high in the upper mist, they had glimpses of the fighting mare, and of Tombstone clinging like a shipwrecked man.

Something hit the ground, slithering sidewise, ploughing up the dust. With the last flopping turn it appeared as the body of a man. The clothes were white with dust. The face was black with it.

Up on the veranda the girl screamed, but no one turned to look towards her. She had not screamed because Tombstone was on the ground, sprawling. The cry came from her when she saw Montana leave the fence as a puma leaves a bough for a kill.

To the men who watched, close up, the similarity was even greater. They saw the devouring hunger in the eyes of Montana. They saw him crouching, gripping the top rail of the fence with both hands. The next moment he was plunging through the dust that smoked across the face of the corral. They saw him dodging through it while the wild mare tried to flee from him— as though she feared tooth and claw.

He caught her like that, too. As she swerved out of a corner he leaped at her with hands and feet. She soared. He appeared gripping the pommel with one hand, the rest of him streaming upwards. But a moment later he was in the saddle.

The dust billowed like fog struck by a sea wind; the mare was the wind. They had glimpses of her red mouth gaping, the sheen of her wild eyes. They saw her high up, fighting thin air. They heard her strike the ground again and again, the shadowy form of the rider shocked and snapped to either side. By a single foot, a single hand, he seemed to be clinging half the time—as if with talons that hooked into tender flesh.

The watchers were frozen in place because it was not a riding contest. There was death in the air. Tombstone Joe leaned on the fence with his face dripping blood, and black, clotted dust.

The yelling had ended.

Each cowpuncher retained his past position. One was on one knee. Another, on tiptoe, gripped the top of a post and seemed to be yelling, though no sound came. Another held his hat rigidly above his head, but forgot to wave it.

And from the veranda it could be seen that the head of Montana, at every impact, wavered crazily up and down. His chin was beating on his breast. At every lurch of the mare he seemed about to shoot from the saddle, but something stuck him in place. Luck, men might have called it. But it was not luck.

The man or the mare would fall dead, surely.

Then she staggered and stood still, her legs braced wide apart.

After a time, Montana got slowly down from the saddle. He slid down. His face was crimson. Blood from his mouth, his ears, his nose, had covered his face

28

with a red mask. He felt his way to the head of the mare. He put his arm around her neck. He began to stroke her face.

And she, with half-closed eyes of exhaustion, leaned slowly against him. He pulled out his bandana. Instead of drying his own frightful face, he began to wipe the slobber and the froth from the muzzle of Sally.

CHAPTER IV

It was only a few days after this that Mateo Rubriz sat in a *cantina* in "Greaser Town," the Mexican adjunct of Bentonville, near the Lavery ranch. Good Brother Pascual had left the table as soon as he had finished his dish of hot frijoles. There remained only Mateo Rubriz and a sallow-faced man with high, squared shoulders such as one expects to see only in a soldier. He looked like an army officer—and a consumptive. He wore the garb of a prosperous Mexican *charro*, all yellow leather and a starring of silver that brightened and waned as he turned in his chair or lifted his glass to drink the green-white tequila.

He was Jack Lascar. Everyone south of the border knew him, and everyone north of the river knew him; but no one knew his nationality. Some people said that he was in fact a Lascar. They looked at the yellow whites of his eyes and said that.

He carried with him an air of amused superiority. He retained this air as he said:

"If I walk into the street and tell people that Mateo Rubriz is in here—if I tell the gringos that—what'll they do to you, Rubriz?"

Mateo Rubriz grinned. A stiff wave of flesh rose up from his cheeks and almost obscured his eyes. He leaned forward.

"Your father——" he began.

After that, his voice was so soft that Jack Lascar had to bend his head to hear the words. A dreamy expression came over the face of Lascar.

"That's what I always wanted to know," said Lascar. "I always wanted to know who cut him down. It was you?"

"Who else would have dared?" asked Rubriz, leaning back, with a two-handed gesture of triumph.

Jack Lascar grunted. "Then what do you want?" he asked.

"I want you to accept a favour," said the Mexican.

"Humph!" grunted Lascar again. "Well?"

"You hate one man a good deal."

"Do I?"

"The Montana Kid?"

Jack Lascar turned a little in his chair, quickly. He glanced over his shoulder at the door. He looked at the window, also. Then he finished the white fire of his tequila and stared at Rubriz.

"Damn him!" said Jack Lascar.

"Once, in Nevada, in Carson City, in the Imperial Saloon," began Rubriz, "on a Tuesday morning——"

"Damn *you!*" said Lascar.

Rubriz leaned back in his chair. He looked, at that moment, like a fat, rather soft man of middle age, a pulpy creature half-rotted by time. But Jack Lascar knew otherwise.

"This Montana Kid," said Rubriz, "is a man who would come to a challenge like a dog to raw meat. Now, if you write out a challenge in English—can you write English?"

"I write five languages," said Lascar, slowly, bitterly. "And I punch cows for a damned——"

"Gringo," suggested Rubriz, still smiling.

Jack Lascar was silent.

Then Rubriz said:

"If you wrote out a challenge and nailed it on the post-office notice board, the town would know it. The

Kid would know it. He would come. And the sheriff he is not in town. The law is not in town. It is away —for one whole day!"

Jack Lascar lighted a cigarette. He held out his glass. The keeper of the *cantina* came running in whispering slippers. He filled the glass until drops ran over on to the floor. Lascar slopped the drink into his mouth. A part of it drizzled down his chin and dropped on to the yellow bright leather of his costume, unheeded. He did not even wipe his face as he continued to stare at Rubriz.

"The Montana Kid would come!" said Rubriz.

"He would not come!" said Jack Lascar. "Everybody knows, even the little babies know, that if Montana ever pulls a gun and shoots at another man—even in self-defence—the sheriff will be on his trail with a posse."

Rubriz closed his eyes to keep the fire in them from being seen. It was his plan, his whole plan—to tear Montana away from the land of the gringos by putting on a seeming break with the law. After that, where was there for him to flee except into Mexico? And with whom would he travel so readily as with Mateo Rubriz? And, once on the road, would not the robbing of the fort at Duraya be to El Keed no more than the drinking of a glass of whisky? If only this Jack Lascar could be used as the lure!

"No matter what he fears," said Rubriz, "he fears shame more. You know that I have a good reason to curse him?"

"He stole away your son," Jack Lascar sneered. "He took your son, and carried him away, and made him a gringo."

"He did," said Rubriz, with an immense calm which was not an affectation. "That is the reason why he must die."

He meant that. No matter what friendship lay

32

between them, for that deed, one day, El Keed must die. And Rubriz, staring out the window at the red dying of the day, breathing the sharp, stale scent of cigarette smoke, looking across the little round, iron tables, went on:

"I cannot challenge him, because I cannot appear. As soon as I show myself in the streets, the people rise up in a wave and wash me away into a jail. But *you* can challenge him. You can name the hour. You can stand in the middle of the street and wait, while everyone wonders that any man could have the courage to wait for El Keed in a fair fight. How will they know that Mateo Rubriz lies in hiding beside one of the houses, or inside a window, with a rifle aimed and ready to end the fight before it begins? Do you hear, Jack? El Keed will be dead before he has a chance to become an outlaw again! He will be dead before he has a chance to run away from the law."

CHAPTER V

SUNDAY morning on the Lavery ranch found the Montana Kid moving about in his room with a slight limp, but whistling at the work of incasing his long body and his strong shoulders in white shirt and collar, in socks of black silk, and in a fine blue-black serge, at last. One thing he would not do—he would not change boots for shoes. But unless his trousers were hitched up, no one could tell that boots of softest, most highly-polished calf were what he wore. For they were not the high-heeled pinch-toes of the usual cowpuncher. If the horse dropped under Montana, he could not afford to be hobbled by tight boots; he had to land like a running cat into which sundry enemies of his had seen him transformed more than once. Even as he knotted his necktie on his wedding day, he kept flexing his feet a little in the softness of those boots because he could not tell what guns might look at him before this day was ended. It was what he most disliked—an advertised appearance; and there were plenty of men in the world who might want to take advantage of it. He would need three pairs of eyes with which to keep on guard this day; but that was what he had needed a great part of his life, and perhaps it was why he was whistling now.

His stay on the Lavery ranch had been a quiet back-water, a pause in the hurry of the current that was headed towards some wild and unknown sea. Now that he was dressed, he looked quizzically at the brown face in the mirror and found that the blue-bright eyes were alert for danger rather than for happiness.

Grey-headed Ransome, the foreman, poured tight and helpless into Sunday clothes, smoked a cigarette and watched the procedure of his friend. "It'll be a great day," said Ransome.

"A long day," corrected the Kid.

"Any bozo might think," suggested Ransome, "that you wasn't gunna step out with a beauty that had a coupla millions to float her."

"Might any bozo think that?" murmured Montana.

"Any bozo might think," went on Ransome, heavily, frowning, "that you didn't give much of a damn about one of the prettiest girls in the world."

Montana turned. There was a certain speed and luxurious leisure combined in his movements, like the juggler who lets not the flash but the pausing of his hands be seen. Ransome stood up as though danger threatened him; and perhaps danger did. But though the temper of the Kid was as quick as the stroke of a startled diamond-back, his friendship was a force as unalterably persistent as gravity. And Ransome was his friend. So the foreman went on:

"Montana, I don't care if you get sore. I'm gunna tell you what I think. You were pretty fond of Mrs. Lavery. After she died, you begun to find this here ranch sort of cramped. It wasn't no pasture for a mustang like you. It wasn't a box stall, even. You've got so tired of the Lavery ranch that you're tired of the girl, too, before you marry her!"

The Kid, instead of answering, looked at Ransome with eyes that had become the colour of slate; then he picked up that pair of Colts with the extra long barrels and made it disappear inside his clothes with one of those swift, easy gestures which the eye could not follow very well. After that he went to Ransome and laid a light touch on his shoulder.

"Old Ransome!" he said.

"Yeah, old Ransome be damned," said the foreman. "What about old Montana, I'm asking?"

Many other things were going on at the same time about the big Lavery house. There was Ruth Lavery in her room, being draped in films of white. She smiled a good deal until the girl who was the best of her friends said to her, suddenly, whispering:

"Ruth, are you smiling because you're happy, or just to please me?"

"I'm happy, of course," answered Ruth Lavery. "But I'm frightened. Something is going to happen!"

And in front of the house Richard Lavery, senior, was walking restlessly up and down, up and down, scanning the horizon from time to time as though he expected a sign of changing weather to roll darkly up on the edge of the world.

He turned almost expectantly towards a sudden rattle of hoofs that beat on the lower trail and then revealed a rider on a sweating mustang. It was a young fellow with a look of anxiety, as though wild Indians might be behind him. He threw himself out of the saddle and ran to Lavery.

"D'you know what's happened?" he gasped. "Jack Lascar—that yaller-faced feller called Lascar that showed up in town the other day—he's gone and nailed a notice on the bulletin-board in front of the post office. I've copied it down!"

He pulled out a piece of paper and read aloud. Half the words were a gasping whisper and half were almost shouted.

"Everybody notice that wants to:

"Me, that is Jack Lascar, is going to stand out in the middle of the street in front of Hi Bailey's blacksmith shop at ten-thirty this same morning and wait for the low yaller hound by name of Montana Kid.

"If he don't show up then and there, you all know what kind of a skunk he is.

(Signed)
"JACK LASCAR."

"Wait a moment," exclaimed Lavery. "Where's the sheriff? What does he mean by permitting open challenges in a place like Bentonville?"

"The sheriff's out of town," said the messenger. "Some of the boys have sent for him. He ought to be back by about ten-thirty. But I thought that you might want to know——"

"Get off the ranch!" cried Lavery. "Don't let Montana see you. If he should find out——"

He found that the rounded eyes of the messenger were peering straight past him and, turning, Richard Lavery saw Montana standing in the open door of the house. Above the white of the stiff collar his face looked browner and younger than ever. Montana was rolling a cigarette, letting his fingers see their own way, while he said:

"You ride back and tell Jack Lascar that it's a little late for me to get his message, but I'm coming down there as fast as a good horse will take me. Tell him that I'll finish the job I left half done a while back."

He scratched the match, touched the flame to the crimped end of the wheat-straw paper, and took in a good, deep breath of the smoke. His eyes had an absent look, as though he were considering a further answer. But the messenger jerked his head in under-

37

standing and ran back to his pony. It was something worth remembering during a life to be the connecting link between a Jack Lascar and a Montana.

The Kid started for the corrals. As for Lavery, he made a few steps in pursuit; then he paused and lifted an arm and parted his lips, but the words did not come. Instead, he turned and made for the house. He walked with short steps, like a man stiffened with anger.

The Kid, in the small corral nearest the big barn, went out to the blood-bay mare that he had christened Sally. She fled for a moment like a bird with a hawk overhead, but presently she stood still and laughed at the man and her own fear, with her bright eyes. For they had become new friends, but very deep friends, since the day of their fight to a finish. Montana led her by the mane into the saddle-shed. Already his serge suit was dusted over with white. But there was no time to change. Even as things stood, he would have to travel fast to get to Bentonville by ten-thirty.

When he got into the saddle and jogged around the corner of the barn he saw that he would have to face all the music in one great burst. A whole picture of disapproval had been painted for him. For on the veranda stood the assembled family down to the one-legged cook, with a shimmer of white for Ruth Lavery in the centre of the group, and her father tall and straight and forbidding beside her.

Montana rode straight up to them and pulled off his hat.

"I've got the call that a man has to answer, Ruth," he said.

She only stared at him. Her lips were parted a little. She looked older; she seemed to be squinting at a bright, distant light. The future, as like as not. Montana tried to feel sorry, but couldn't.

Richard Lavery did the speaking. He said:

"This will be about all, my lad. My girl has put up with a good bit. She's put off the wedding because of a hunting trip you wanted to go on; and then because you had to chase a wild horse; and now you're going down to face the challenge of a poisonous bit of scum called Jack Lascar. You'll forget about him here and now, or else you'd better forget about Ruth."

Montana dismounted. The "wild" mare started to follow him up the steps, but shrank away from these strangers. Her master stood over Ruth.

"He's speaking for you, I suppose?" said Montana. But she only kept on staring. One could not say whether there was more pain or fear in her eyes.

"It appears that I *am* speaking for her," said Lavery. "We know what we owe to you, but there's a future as well as a past to think of."

"Wait a minute," said Montana. "You can only talk for yourself. Say something, Ruth!"

"I can't," she answered. "If I try to talk—I'll only be weeping."

"People cry about things that are gone, finished. Am I finished as far as you're concerned?"

She shook her head.

"I gave you a promise about the riding of the mare, and then I broke it. Does that make you feel that you can never trust me?"

"Do you trust yourself?" she asked.

This struck him very hard, apparently. He began to reason on her side:

"It's our wedding day—and I ride off—I'll always be riding off. Is that what you feel?"

She was silent.

"I know," concluded Montana. "I can see it. What's left in you is mostly fear."

"I want to be braver and bigger," said the girl, "but I can't help it. Why are you this way?"

"Because the devil got into me between breaths, I suppose," said Montana. "You won't believe how my heart's aching for you now. You seem to me everything that's right and beautiful. If I go away, the best half of the world will be behind me. But I can't stay and be the happy cat by the fire. Even thinking of that drives me crazy. In the middle of the night something would catch me by the hair of the head and yank me a thousand miles away into some sort of trouble. If we had children, you'd be counting them orphans two or three times a year. Ruth, I'm going away. . . . No matter what happens to-day, there's no coming back for me."

He took her suddenly in his arms. The tears began to run down her face, but she said, very gently:

"I'm not pitying myself. It's for you! I think God pities you, too—and loves you."

She lifted her face and he kissed her.

Then he turned to Lavery and shook hands.

"I was hating you a minute ago—but you're right," he said.

"There'll be another chance for me to show you that I'll never forget you," said Lavery. "If you'll still listen to me, I'll still beg you——"

He checked himself. His unspoken words filled a beating moment of silence, and then Montana was walking jauntily down the steps and waving his hand.

"So long, everyone," he called.

Ransome started making a mumbling sound, but he kept changing his mind about the words he intended to speak, so that none of them was clear. Only the cook shouted out, as the Kid mounted:

"I wish to God I had two legs under me, and I'd ride with you, Montana!"

Afterwards, as he sat the saddle, he heard Ruth crying:

"But he'll be killed! Father, he's going to be——"

The sudden beating of the hoofs of the red mare drowned out that complaint. As he came to the turn of the road, he felt an invisible hand tugging at his shoulder and therefore he turned in the saddle and rode out of view with his hat waving over his head.

Well, the girl feared him more than she loved him; and he loved her less than he feared a housed life. To see the spring and the summer and the winter show their faces always at the same spots, that was as forbidding to Montana as the thought of a prison cell might be to other men.

Now the house was out of view behind him. He let the red mare race to get through the pass between the hills, pointing towards far-off Bentonville. After that he felt that he had slipped the hand of the past from his shoulder. He began to laugh like a child. He had not realized how he had dreaded double harness until he was started on the empty trail again!

CHAPTER VI

IT was ten-twenty by his watch when he headed into the main street of Bentonville. That was cutting the time a bit short, perhaps, but he did not want to burn up the strength of Sally with too hard a run. For, supposing that he met Lascar and survived the fight with him, he might need all the speed that was in the mare immediately. Gun-fights were barred in Bentonville. A message had been sent to the sheriff, who was probably running a horse at a dead gallop to get back to the town in time to prevent this duel. And that same sheriff, solemnly, with careful words, had warned Montana that a single flash of a gun in his hand would be enough to land him in jail.

"This here new reputation of yours," said the sheriff, "is a lot of pretty light stuff. There's plenty of honest citizens that claim you ought to be doin' time in the penitentiary right now. This here reputation—why, it's so much dry powder, and one spark is gunna blow it to hell, and you along with it. No matter where your feet carry you, mind what your hands do after you walk into trouble. Maybe the other fellow will be to blame, but you're the one that'll go to jail."

It was curious, in a way, that Jack Lascar should have called for a show-down—a public show-down. Because there was nothing public about the character or the past of Jack. He loved twilight and twilight ways like a cat. A fight at midday in the middle of a street was not the usual procedure for Jack. One would expect rather a knife in the back, a bullet from behind. The man had plenty of skill and plenty of courage, but he used his talents like a red Indian. There was some mystery behind this challenge—or was it that the memory of that other defeat, that public shaming, had driven Jack Lascar into a frenzy at last, until death was better than a life in which men smiled behind his back?

A freckle-faced boy ran out from a yard and at the side of Montana:

"Are you gunna do it, Montana?" he shrilled. "Are you gunna kill him? The sheriff'll chase you if you pull a gun in this town! Don't get yourself chased away from us, Montana. Everybody knows you licked Lascar once. Everybody knows you ain't afraid!"

"Things will be all right, thanks, brother," said the Kid.

The boy, panting, drew off to the side, shaking his head; and then settled down into a steady dog-trot to get to the appointed place of the meeting.

The street unrolled itself before Montana's eyes. He saw it as the sign of the old life which was returning to him. He smiled at the saloon signs. Behind them were long, cool rooms with the sour of beer and the sweet of whisky in the air, and further to the rear were the smaller chambers where card games were generally in progress. In his gambling he preferred the crooked experts, partly because their pockets were always more full of money, partly because he never enjoyed winning from the weak, and above all because equal chances made a keener fight that was worth the winning. But those back rooms had offered a hundred adventures in the Odyssey of his life.

The General Merchandise Store could outfit him for the desert or the mountains. In the blacksmith shops there were hands cunning in a thousand contrivances.

But, above all, behind this quiet village life, or stirring through it, were men of the right stuff, the hard fibre.

Then he saw Hi Bailey's blacksmith shop in the distance, thin blue wisps of smoke leaking out through the big, open doors of the place. No horses were tethered in front of it, waiting their turn to be shod. Instead, the string was hitched on the near side of the place. Well, if bullets were to fly, horseflesh is as penetrable as the bodies of men, but the Kid knew himself and he knew Jack Lascar. There would be no wild shots in this fight!

No wonder the rest of the town had seemed deserted. All the life of it was concentrated here. The windows, the doorways, were filled, and people stood at the corners of the houses. A dull murmur rose, swelled into a many-throated voice. The rumbling came from men. The women and children gave the shrill to the sound. And then the Kid was touched with scorn and with anger.

"Good" people are a queer lot. These fellows who were gathered as such eager spectators for a fight would also ride, at the sheriff's call, hot foot down the trail of the winner. The Kid smiled and without mirth.

He looked down and saw that he was white with dust. He had stuffed the trousers into the tops of his boots and dust was thick in the folds beneath the knee. City clothes, like city people, were foolish things, without the free flow of a range outfit or of range men. He made two deft, imperceptible gestures that assured him of the positions of his guns.

Then he saw a slender figure walk slowly out from under an awning and step into the street with feet that lifted high, as though this man did not wish to kick the dust up over the polish of his boots.

That was Jack Lascar. His bright Mexican jacket flashed dazzling in the sun.

"I'll put a red spot on that jacket," said Montana, softly.

He dismounted. The mare followed him, shying a bit from side to side as she kept seeing fresh crowds of humans on either side of the street.

Lascar stood in the exact centre of the street, with his hands on his hips. There was no wind to furl back the wide brim of his hat and let Montana see the darkened face beneath. If he had more light on the face, he would try his shot for the head. Well, he might try for the head, anyway. The bright buckle of the hat-belt would be a neat target—neat and small. And the rather bad chances of Jack Lascar would be evened a little.

Someone yelled:

"Hurry it up! Hurry it up! The sheriff's comin', hell bent!"

Then out of the distance Montana could hear the small beating of hoofs.

Jack Lascar had turned sidewise. He was not fool enough to offer the full breadth of his body to an enemy. He forgot that this turn brought the buckle of the hat-belt into fuller view.

They were twenty paces apart.

"How does this suit you, Jack?" asked Montana.

Lascar's whole body jerked with the violence of his words. He barked his curses like a dog. Any distance suited him. Ten paces would be better.

The Kid smiled and walked straight on.

A woman screeched through the thick silence that covered the town:

"It's gotta be stopped! It's murder! Two of God's creatures out there to murder——"

The voice was muffled. A man could be heard to say, distinctly:

"Now, Mame, don't you go bein' a fool. The boys have gotta have their fun, don't they?"

The hoofbeats from the rear must have rounded a corner. They seemed suddenly nearer. It seemed to be a signal for Jack Lascar. The man seemed hungry for the battle as he jerked out a gun.

The Kid made his draw in midstep. He fired as his foot struck the ground. Jack Lascar fired one bullet into the air as he spun around. He fell neither forward nor back, but in a heap, and the dust washed up around him as though the earth were anxious to claim its own at once.

CHAPTER VII

With the fall of Jack Lascar there came out of the watchers a deep, quick, animal sound. The lips of men and women and children grinned back suddenly as though there were something in the sight that filled them with a food of satisfaction, or of horror. After that first grunting noise came the babel of spoken words and an uneasy movement forward.

The Kid went up to the body of Lascar and put his foot brutally on the shoulder of the man, and pushed him back so that he sprawled face up. Then Montana could see that a trickle of blood was still running down the side of Lascar's head—sure proof that the fellow was not dead as yet. Well, if that bullet had glanced, it meant that there would be more trouble, great trouble, ahead of Montana. For a man like this, with the courage to face him in the open public, made an enemy worth much consideration.

There was something more to be considered, just now. That was the persistent beating of hoofs down the street and now rounding the last corner. So the Kid jumped Sally, looking back as he jammed his feet into the stirrups. And he saw the sheriff come grandly around the next bend of the street with his mustang aslant, the dust spilling out sidewise from the slashing hoofs, and the wind of the gallop furling back the brim of the sheriff's hat. There was patience, kindness, understanding in the face of this man of the law, and he had shown all of these qualities in his dealing with Montana long before. There was also a bulldog persistence and

47

that sort of courage which is found in a man who loves duty more than glory.

And as the sheriff saw the picture before him, the dust still rising above the place where Jack Lascar lay, the man of the law shouted. His cry was like the hoarse bark of a sea lion as he went for his gun.

Montana did not try to get away down the street. Neither did he open fire on the sheriff, because it was not his habit to shoot at the law-abiding. Instead, he sent the mare winging over a four-foot fence and then crashing through tall shrubbery that closed over man and horse like water. The sheriff's bullets crackled through the brush; other bullets sang a smaller and a higher note around the ears of Montana.

He looked up and saw a rifleman seated on the very ridge of a roof. The fellow had gone up to get a perfect view of the meeting between Montana and Lascar. He had carried his gun with him in case there was a chance for him to put in his hand safely at the end of the fight.

The lips of the Kid twitched back from his teeth.

There are a lot of people in the world who need killing! But now he had to swerve the mare on to a back lane, and send her scooting. There was going to be plenty of trouble. He could hear the voice of it growl and howl through Bentonville.

The lions had finished fighting, and now the spectators would take part in a lion-hunt. Horses began to snort and squeal under the spur as men mounted and drove away in the pursuit. Men yelled orders in voices that squeaked with excitement. There was even a sudden discharge of three or four shots that could not have been aimed at anything.

The Kid smiled a little. His eyes filled with reminiscent pleasure. He knew all the instruments in this orchestra. He had heard them many times before. And the music assured him that he was out of the drowsy noontide of the commonplace and back in the chill wind of the world of adventure.

From his position, the south trail was the best trail. He went straight for it, taking note how the mare carried her head high, moving it in observation, keeping her ears pricked. She was iron-hard. The run from the ranch had not weighted her hoofs with the least weariness. Even if she had found a master and flown at last to a lure, she was still strong from those wild years of winging through the wilderness. He felt that he had caught from the sky something that would carry him safely away from any earthbound dangers.

The last house, the last barn, whirled away behind him. He was heading towards the beginning of the south trail with the tumult of Bentonville drawing to a single head behind him, when he saw a man on a black horse riding furiously down the northern slope to head him off.

There was still time to turn to the left down a broken ravine, but though he might avoid one enemy in this manner, he would leave himself trapped for that purring crowd whose horses were beating up a thunder behind him. Besides, he was in no mood to turn for one man or for two. So he drew a gun.

The mare flowed beneath him like the current of a river; to shoot from her back would be as easy as shooting from the deck of a ship. But then he saw that the stranger had neither drawn a revolver nor unsheathed the rifle whose holster slanted down under the right leg of the rider. It was a brown-faced Mexican, in overalls, with a tattered rag of a hat fluttering on his head. He was dressed like a peon, though he rode a horse fit for a king. Something in that contrast, and in the thick solidity of the fellow's shoulder, put knowledge in the eyes of the Kid.

"Rubriz!" he shouted.

He got a wild yell and the wave of an arm for answer. It was Rubriz himself who pulled on to the trail beside him, checking the great black horse with a cruel Mexican bit that wrenched open the mouth of the stallion.

"Welcome! Well seen, El Keed!" cried Rubriz. "But take another way than this. The whole town is on horseback. They've seen me and they're chasing me. Some dog of a spy has warned them that I'm north of the Rio Grande!"

The shouted Mexican speech was music in the ears of Montana. If he added up the happiness of his life, half of it, and the spicier half, he had found in the land of that tongue. He smiled as he answered:

"They hunt *me*, Mateo!"

"They hunt you? Then they hunt us both!" answered Rubriz.

He turned in his saddle. Montana knew what the Mexican was seeing—the first riders out of Bentonville, lashing or spurring their horses, riding a race with the wicked joy of the man-hunt maddening their hearts. What Montana looked at were the gross, powerful lines of the Mexican and the white scar of the whip-lash across his face. It would not have surprised him if, at this meeting, the bandit had leaped for his throat. Neither did it surprise him that Rubriz was ready to fight and die with him. The smile of Montana became a laugh.

"They are coming like ten thousand devils!" shouted Rubriz, turning front again. "San Juan of Capistrano, lame their horses, throw sand in their eyes. Hai, Montana! We ride our first trail together. They can never catch us. Not this black and not the mare— but I have a poor friend down the trail a few miles with only a mule to carry him. No horse would have the patience to carry the bulk of him. Look—there!—there! See him lumbering the mule, flopping his elbows!"

Far in the distance Montana saw a figure that was huge even when it was far away—a long-robed friar on a jogging mule. The arms of the man flopped like clipped wings; his head was bare to that powerful sun.

There was only a glimpse before a turn of the trail snatched the figure from view.

"They'll never harm a friar," said Montana. "He's safe enough."

"No Mexican is safe, not even if there were a halo instead of a hat on his head," answered Rubriz. "But how shall we save him? How shall we snatch him away? Aha! He sees trouble behind him at last!"

The friar had in fact halted his mule, which turned sidewise as the rider stared behind him at the two fugitives and that rising dust-cloud from under which the horses of the men from Bentonville were darting.

"Save yourself, thick-skull! Help yourself out of the way, half-wit!" shouted Rubriz, angrily.

The man was much too far away to hear, but, as though he knew the meaning of Rubriz, he stared first into the depths of the gorge that fenced the trail on one side and then looked helplessly up the steep slope of the hill which was littered with a vast strewing of boulders, big and small.

Another bend of the trail again shut out the view of the friar, but when he was seen again, he had dismounted from the mule, which was picking at grass beside the trail, while the master clambered actively over the rocky junk-heap of the slope, looking too big to be human, against the sky.

"That's the best way for him," said Rubriz. "What's he at, now? Run on, fool! Run on and save your hide!"

For the friar was seen heaving at the boulders on the slope. There he laboured as Rubriz and Montana went by, the Mexican rising in his stirrups to screech: "Run, brother! Pascual, run for your life!"

For answer, a stentorian shout rolled down the hill, and Montana had sight of a flashing smile and a brown-black face. Then, bending to his work again, the friar toppled a boulder of several hundredweight. It swayed; it staggered. It began to hop down the hill with increasing bounds, and wherever it struck it loosened a mass of other huge rocks until the hillside became alive. The thunder of the rocks quite shut out the hoof beats of the posse. Only thin, screaming voices of dismay came wavering through the air above the tumult of the landslide.

Brother Pascual was already hurrying down to the trail, where he remounted his mule and jogged on after the other two, while behind him the boulders still skipped and danced, hurtling down the trail with force that chewed great portions out of the lip of the rock; the overflow made a cataract of thunder into the bottom of the ravine and set the echoes rolling. The whole slope, above, seemed to be in motion, a river of down-flooding stone, and even when it stopped rushing, how could the men of the town climb their horses over those vast blocks which now obstructed the way?

The delight of Rubriz was like that of a child. He laughed till the tears were rolling on his face.

"Where's the fool who denies the power of prayer?" he demanded. "There's Brother Pascual, as simple as a sheep, but he's sharpened his wits by arguing with the saints and gossiping with the angels till he's able to think of a trick like that. You and I can do a few little things, but it takes a man of God to move mountains Montana!"

Here the friar came up with them and, in response to a few words from Rubriz, took the hand of Montana in a vast, slow, and long-continued pressure, while his doubting eyes seemed to be struggling to grapple with the soul of the Kid at the same time.

"Here's three of us that make one man," said Rubriz, "and while we're together, let's see the mountain we can't fly over and the river we can't jump across."

CHAPTER VIII

THEY came to the verge of the Rio Grande, where the yellow currents flattened out to a shallow width that a rider could ford easily. There they dismounted as Montana said:

"I turn north here, Mateo. I can travel in peace, now, thanks to Brother Pascual."

"*Adios, amigo,*" answered Rubriz. "Now I look on you for the last time; and while I live I shall remember you."

"The last time?" asked Montana.

"I go now on a trail from which I can never return," said Rubriz, cheerfully.

"What trail is that?" asked Montana.

He noted that Brother Pascual, with a troubled face, was retreating from them.

"Our Lady calls to me," said Rubriz, waving towards the horizon. "The task she asks is more than one man can do; but I must go."

Montana sat down on a rock and lighted a cigarette.

"I'm ready to listen. There's no hurry," he said, looking around him at the broken steps of the canyon, at the yellow workings of the current.

Rubriz made a great sound, clearing his throat and scowling, to cover his satisfaction. And he told, striding up and down, how in the town of Duraya the governor's fort on the hill stares across at the big church of Our Lady of Guadalupe. He told of the little Bishop Emiliano, with a head as bald as a polished stone, fringed around with silver. He told of General Estrada,

54

the governor—of his huge brush of a moustache and his rapacious eyes, which could only find devastation and poverty in his new province until he heard of the restoration of the emerald crown of Our Lady to the church from which it had been stolen. He told of the fight in the church, the felling of the bishop, the savage stand of the great friar, and that despairing call for help which Brother Pascual had brought into the mountains.

"So I knew that I must make the try," he finished. "One man to enter the fort? I could never come back. Before I died, I wanted to see you once more, *amigo*. I could not tell what I would do when I saw you. I might want to draw a knife and try for your throat, or I might see a brother in you. Well, I saw you—and I did not want to draw a knife."

He stood over the Montana Kid and smiled down at him with an unaffected admiration and fondness. He held out his hand, saying:

"Then, *adios*, Montana!"

The Kid failed to see the hand. He made a gesture with his cigarette.

"Wait a minute," he said. "I get things mixed up, down there in Mexico. Duraya—let's see—it's in the loop of a river, eh?"

"The river runs almost all the way around it," agreed Rubriz.

"The fort has big stone walls, like those of a castle in the old days?"

"Just so!"

"And down the hill from the fort there's a *cantina* run by Miguel Santos—a man who looks like a *caballero*. But he has a wooden leg that's pulled him down in the world."

"I know the man," agreed Rubriz. "What about him?"

"Nothing about him. But there's a flash of a girl in that *cantina*. She keeps a red rose in the black of her hair. The *charros* look at her and forget how their tequila tastes. They drink it like water while she's around. Her name—her name is Rosita."

"There is such a girl," agreed Rubriz.

Montana stood up, threw away his cigarette.

"Thank God for an eye which can remember! Mateo, I am riding to Duraya with you."

"No, my friend!" protested the Mexican. "There is danger for you, south of the River. The Rurales remember you. They would smell out your trail as if they were bloodhounds. They would be at your throat in a day."

"Mateo, I must go to Duraya. I must see that girl Rosita again. There was something about her that seemed to say, 'Come once more. I shall remember.' Besides, I want to see the moustache of General Estrada."

"You don't know what you say!" protested Rubriz. "This Estrada is a man who knows his business. He keeps his soldiers as lean as wolves. Their teeth are in you before you know it."

"Mateo, tell me in a word. Do you want me to help you get the emeralds? Do you want me to steal 'em with you, or not? Could you trust the treasure of the church in the hands of a gringo?"

"Ah, brother!" said Rubriz. "You and I together we could walk even through the walls of the fort at Duraya! But how can I repay you, Montana? What can I do for El Keed?"

"You can teach me, while we are on the road, a song that I may sing for Rosita. I tell you, Mateo, I've always known in my blood that I would see her again. And she knows that I'll come. Here, give me your hand! This is the meaning—that we shall never part till we've won the emeralds for the little bishop with the bald head. Come, Rubriz! Is the friar in this, too? Come here, Brother Pascual. Now, all three of us, with our hands crossed—so! And the man who falls away from this promise, why, he's a dog, and he'll rot with the mange! To horse, now, and over the river!"

But, as their hands parted, the big friar held the other two men motionless in a strange way; for he lifted his hands above their heads and seemed to grow with that gesture into a veritable giant. With upraised face he prayed, silently.

Mateo and the Kid, like shamefaced children, pulled off their hats and let the blessing fall.

The friar walked or ran most of the way south; and he seemed to spend more energy pulling the mule after him than in getting his own bulk over the ground. Only when the way was level and there was a chance for a lope or a brisk trot would he step into the saddle and ride the mule through the dust which the horses raised.

"Why does he do it?" asked Montana.

"Once a mule that was carrying him through the mountains slipped on a frozen rock and broke its leg," answered Rubriz. "Since then he takes pity on four-legged beasts. I had to stamp and rage to make him ride, on the way north with me. Even then he would not take a horse. A mule was too good for him, he said. You see, he is but a child."

"A child that moves mountains, eh?" said Montana. "But why did he come north with you?"

"He had heard the thousand stories about you, brother. He was hungry to see your face. That will make him a great man with the shepherds and the villagers."

"Ah! So that was the reason!" murmured Montana.

But though he smiled, the first doubt had entered his soul, coldly. He saw that he would have to be on his guard from now on.

As they came through the hills into view of Duraya, the sunset flared and died quickly. It made the white walls of the town bloom for a moment. It made the looping river run red. Then the soft twilight rose out of the valleys, overflowed the hills, invaded the sky, and brought down the stars.

They descended into the plain.

"You tell me, Brother Pascual," said Montana. "Shall I pass as a true Mexican cowboy?"

"Why not, dear friend?" asked the friar. "Your hair is black. And now that you have rubbed a little of that stain into your skin, you are as dark as most. Your hair is already black, and as for the blue eyes, those are found in Mexico often enough. Besides, the red mare is the sort of horse that a famous *charro* would ride. And you have a suit of yellow leather with silver spangles all over it. The good Mexican speech comes so easily off your tongue that even I, who know, at times forget the truth about you."

"Tell me, also," said Montana, laughing, "if you think that you could ever really open your heart to a gringo."

After a long pause the friar said:

"I can at least try, my friend. All men are the children of one God. So I can at least try!"

CHAPTER IX

In Duraya they separated.

The friar went to the church. But the bishop was not there. So he went to the bishop's palace and climbed the stairs which were open and unguarded day and night in order that the poorest of the poor might come to Bishop Emiliano in the little, upper room which was all that he reserved for himself out of the splendours he might have enjoyed. That splendour was disappearing. The gilded chairs and the rich carpets and the pictures, one by one, disappeared and the funds were spent for the relief of the needy. The rich ranchers and the merchants complained that the bishop was turning his palace into a barn. But the poor people loved him and took his love for granted. They came to him complaining as children go to a father.

That was why little Bishop Emiliano, kneeling in prayer with only two candles to light the wooden cross on the naked wall of his room, paid no heed when the friar entered and kneeled in turn. The poor often did this. Rich people need only pray on Sundays and holy days, briefly; but the poor have need to pray every day of their lives. Therefore the destitute or the suffering would climb up the stairs to the bishop's room and kneel in front of his little wooden cross, which was all the symbol of God that appeared in his room. By day or by night they often found him there. If he were busy at other things, nevertheless he would at least pause to speak a few words with them. Sometimes they found him asleep and then, as a rule, they would kneel and face not the cross, but the dim, wan, exhausted face of that good man. And if they came to his room and found that he was not there at all, nevertheless they would stay to make their supplications, for they felt a virtue even in the empty air of the room.

For these reasons, the bishop was not disturbed by the entrance of the friar; he was only vaguely aware that another presence was there, and it was some time before he looked over and found that Brother Pascual had returned to him. He started up at once and went to the kneeling giant.

"Give me your blessing," said the friar, earnestly, without rising.

Even on his knees he was almost as tall as the bishop.

"Give me a blessing of a special grace, for I have done a thing that will bring much evil on my country."

"What thing have you done?" asked the bishop.

"I have helped bring into Mexico a terrible man," said the friar. "I have brought El Keed all the way from the north to Duraya."

"Ah, my son," said the bishop, "why have you done this? That is a known man and a lawbreaker."

"He is a lawbreaker," said the friar, "and in fact he breaks the law so well that Rubriz would not try to steal away the emerald crown of Our Lady unless he had the help of the gringo."

"Are they not great enemies?" asked the bishop. "The story is that the gringo stole away the foster son of Rubriz."

"They are great enemies, but also they love one another," said the friar. "I have seen their lips twitching with distaste and a horror as they looked into each other's eyes, but each man is willing to trust the other with life and death."

"What sort of a man is El Keed?" asked the bishop.

"He is a man swift enough to catch a mountain goat and almost big enough to eat one."

"A great, sour brute?"

"It would be better if he were a sour brute. No, he is a smiling danger. Men cannot help trusting him. The women look as though they were seeing their first man."

"But has he actually come to help Rubriz steal the emeralds?"

"That is why he has come. Partly to steal the emeralds, but more to find trouble and adventure."

"Will he need a large reward, Pascual?"

"The danger he finds will be his reward."

"You speak of a reckless fellow, but not of a bad man, I think," said the little bishop.

"I speak of a fire," said Pascual. "Some men may be able to warm their hands at it, but others will soon be yelling inside the flames."

Mateo Rubriz, at this time, was sitting in the house of a friend at the edge of the town. It was a poor shack of 'dobe with only one room. On a mattress in a corner lay three grimy children, sleeping in spite of the lamplight that shone in their faces. The wife of the family was undressing behind a rag of an old red curtain. Her husband sat at the table with Rubriz. The peon kept smacking his thick lips over his pulque. He looked at his drink with astonished eyes, and with continued amazement stared at his guest. For here sat a fortune in the skin of a man. For information concerning the whereabouts of Mateo Rubriz the Rurales would always pay high; for his actual head they would lay down a fortune; because the worst thorn in the side of their self-respect was the continued life and activity of this prince of robbers. So the peon, Oñate, stared hungrily at his guest, but though Rubriz saw and recognized the look, he was perfectly assured that Oñate, the wife, the three children, would sooner give up their own lives than endanger that of their guest.

Three years before, Oñate had been robbed of his two pack-mules as he was following an obscure trail through the mountains. The mules and the loads of tobacco they were carrying had been swept away by a single young robber. When Oñate, in despair, followed the bandit, the outlaw turned back, attacked the poor carrier, beat him severely, and then went cheerfully on his way. Yet, only a day later Oñate encountered his mules on the trail once more. The loads had not been touched. And the lead ropes were in the hands of Rubriz! It was one of his band that had committed the robbery, not yet knowing that his master would never stoop at small prey.

So, to Oñate, and to Oñate's family, the bandit appeared as a good angel. He could trust them absolutely. They would hardly allow him to spend enough money to buy the very food that he consumed. And they dreaded almost more than they desired the gold piece which he always left behind him when he disappeared.

It was in the house of Oñate that Rubriz had wished to put El Keed also, but Montana refused, point blank.

"You'll lie in a soft bed," said Rubriz, "and you'll sleep sound even after the Rurales are in the room!"

"Well," Montana would answer, "I'd rather wake up and see Rurales than chickens on the rafters and pigs on the floor."

So now he was verging towards the most prosperous *cantina* in the town, and the mare passed like a sheen of red silk through the lamplight that passed out a few steps from door and window. She went daintily, sniffing at the myriad odours of man and cookery and dogs and pigs and chickens that crossed and recrossed in the air, besides that other scent which sometimes made her throw her head high as she perceived the acrid air from the mountain desert blown in from afar.

Her rider sat crosswise, with his left leg thrown over the high pommel of the saddle. He carried under his arm a guitar which he had picked up cheap in a music-shop. Now that it was tuned, he struck out a few soft chords and then let his voice start ringing in a very old Spanish song which it would be hard to translate literally. A free rendering, without rhyme, would go something like this:

> "*When the mountains return to the sea*
> *And the throat of the desert is filled,*
> *And between the stars and the ocean*
> *Only the wind is crying,*
> *Then my voice also shall still be heard,*
> *And at the sound of my singing*
> *The stars shall draw closer down*
> *Until they see their faces in the wild water*
> *And hear the name of my beloved:*
> *Rosita! Rosita!*"

That song penetrated into the *cantina* of Miguel Santos, where every chair around the little tables was filled and cigarette butts lay about everywhere on the earthen floor, and the lamplight showed nothing very clearly except the faces of the dirty playing-cards and the lower twists and whirls of smoke. Miguel Santos himself had stepped out from behind his little bar and had gone into the small back room where the more serious games of chance were in progress. Three wild *charros* from far northern Chihuahua were gambling heavily at dice and losing their little fortunes to the house; therefore Miguel Santos smiled a little.

Beyond a certain point of time, no one knew the past of Santos. There was a horrible rumour to the effect that not time, but torment, had worked the evil pattern in the face of Miguel Santos. It was even said, though this was a thing that no one really believed, that he had lost his leg in escaping from the Valley of the Dead. But men did not escape from the Valley of the Dead. It was against chance and against thought that anything human could escape from that well-guarded pit of destruction far in the south, where men and women were made into animals and sold for labour on the tobacco plantations. Women lived there for two years or three. A strong man had been known to endure for as much as seven or eight years. But that was the limit.

Yet if Miguel Santos had not escaped from the Valley of the Dead, then surely he had been through some frightful experience early in his life. He might be fifty now. But twenty years ago, when he first appeared in Duraya, he had appeared almost exactly as old as he was now. He had enough money to open the *cantina*; he had enough money to persuade a pretty girl to marry him. Rosita was born, and her mother died shortly after, not from the effects of the childbirth but because, it was said, she could not endure the ugly torment which was printed for ever in the face of Miguel.

On this night, when he heard the song which ended with the name of Rosita, Miguel Santos instantly left the rear gaming-room and hurried forward, walking with a certain swing which kept the wooden leg in effective motion for long striding. Moving with a peculiar hitch and sway, he could get about almost as well as a normal man of his years.

When he came into the front room he had a mere glimpse of Rosita disappearing through the front door.

"The little bird heard someone whistle," said a tall young *caballero* at one of the tables. Then he laughed, his breath knocking a ragged hole in the smoky air.

Miguel Santos went straight on and through the door into the street. There he saw the mare, the girl, the man. The rider had dismounted. A dim hint of light sparkled over the little silver spangles of his *charro* outfit; the same light gleamed on the red satin of the mare's flank. The eye of Miguel was far sharper than a hawk's when he looked into certain matters. Now he was able to see the wide shoulders, the lofty carriage, the faintly gleaming smile of the man. And he felt the stranger's importance as though the voice of a crier had struck suddenly upon his ear.

"Will you smoke?" the girl was saying.

"Who would light a match in a dark street?" answered the stranger.

Something in the words, something in the voice, clung to the memory of Miguel. He came closer.

"Do you know this *caballero*?" he asked of Rosita.

"Somewhere I have known him," said the girl.

Miguel Santos came so close that he could smell the reek of the sweating horse.

"Who are you?" he asked.

CHAPTER X

THEY went into the little patio of the *cantina*. On one side of the court was the barn and stables to accommodate the horses and mules of travellers. The larger wing was the hotel-saloon. They crossed the enclosure with nothing but starlight to show the way, so Rosita took the hand of Montana and led him. In that manner he was able to pass a broken-down cart, a pile of nameless junk, the kerbstones and wooden top of a well.

Anything might happen here. Out of the dark litter men might start; starlight would hardly show the knives with which all Mexicans know how to work. Once he snatched his hand from the soft fingers of the girl when something moved on the ground. It was only a grunting pig that got out of the way with a voice half deep and half whining. And the girl laughed while Montana slipped back inside his clothes the gun he had drawn.

He left his mare at the foot of an open stair that angled up the wall. Sally rubbed her muzzle against his shoulder. He could see the dim glass of her eyes. She blew out a long breath on him, and stamped, as though to make clear that she did not wish to be left alone in this strange place. But the girl was already a few steps up the stairs, and Montana followed.

At the top landing she pushed open a door. He followed her right into thick darkness. He could hear her breathing, close to him. If this were a trap, the shutting of the door would wall him away forever from the world that had known him. He looked back for an instant into his past and saw the faces of men, savage or laughing, and the broad, comfortable façade of the Lavery home, and Ruth Lavery last of all. But even out of the darkness of this moment he had no regret.

Then a match was scratched. The blue spurt of the flame showed him only the face and the slender hands of the girl, at first. They were the hands of an aristocrat; the touch of them had been so soft that it was plain she had worked most of her life with her smile and her eyes, rather than with her fingers.

The flame burned yellow. He saw a room with two windows, lace curtains across them tied back with yellow ribbons. There was an old four-poster bed. The floor sagged a good bit under the century-old weight of it. A little porcelain stove glittered yellow and white in a corner. The girl was lifting the chimney of a lamp on the table. The flame ran across the wick. A white spot of light sprang out on the ceiling as she pressed the chimney down. The whole room was warmly involved in radiance that let him see all of the girl for the first time. She was blowing out the match, knocking a thin shower of sparks off the charred wood with her breath. Her eyes were down; she was being looked at.

Well, she was worth seeing. She had no place in a room like this. She looked no more at home, here, than a great opera singer doing a one-night stand in the sticks.

"Sit down, señor," said the girl. "My father will come at once. There—you hear him on the stairs?"

Montana heard the bump and pause of sound as the wooden leg laboured up the way. The girl put her head to one side and sighed. She seemed to be pitying the effort of her father, and yet she kept smiling, as though she had learned one lesson so thoroughly that she would never be able to forget it.

"Rosita, you're a dancer, eh?" said he.

"Who has told you that?" she asked him.

"Just because there's a song about you. That old song, Rosita."

"Song?" she echoed, tilting her head.

He sang to her his second song. Although he suppressed the strength of his voice, the resonance vibrated intimately through the room. The meaning of the words ran somewhat like this:

> "You have seen the stream leap,
> And the trout spring in the current,
> And the water-ouzel wing through the spray,
> But I have seen Rosita dancing,
> Dancing, dancing, dancing, dancing.
>
> "You have seen the wind blow out of heaven
> And the leaves whirling round in the wind-pool,
> But you have never laughed with joy,
> Seeing Rosita, Rosita dancing,
> Dancing, dancing, dancing, dancing."

As the first words came from his lips, she began to sway her head a little with the rhythm of the music until the lights quivered along her throat and the rose in her hair nodded a trifle as though in agreement.

The grating knob of the door, as it turned, ended the song and the slight flexion of her accompaniment. Miguel Santos came into the room. He was dressed in white cotton trousers and a clean white apron, but nothing could make him look the part of a bartender. Inside the door he paused for a moment and stared at the stranger. Lines not only seamed the face of Miguel, but also cross-checked it. The closer Montana looked at him, the older he seemed. His eyes were not quite black; they were too bright for that.

"If we are to talk, sit down," said Miguel.

"I never sit down till I'm welcome," said Montana. "I give you first my name and then my errand. My name is José; my errand is to steal from the governor the emerald crown of Our Lady which he took from the church. I have promised Bishop Emiliano to put the crown back in his hands."

These words brought a gasp from the girl; she retreated a little so that she could get a fuller view of the face of the speaker, but the proprietor of the *cantina* was totally unmoved.

He finally said: "Well, then, sit down."

Montana bowed a little to Miguel, a little more to the girl, and took a chair at the round table in the corner of the room. Miguel sat opposite him, his wooden leg squeaking on the floor. The girl leaned her elbows on the back of a chair and kept turning her head from one speaker to the other.

"If the governor learns about you, he burns you alive; if the Rurales learn about you, would they have old scores against you, José?" asked Miguel.

"I never saw one of the Rurales that I would like to sit face to face with," answered Montana, smiling.

He watched the eyes of the other and almost was sure that he saw a slight glitter of answering light in response to this confession.

"Why do you come to me except to get help?" asked Miguel.

"Every man who hates the governor is sure to wish to help me."

"Who tells you that I hate the governor?"

"Every man who loves the bishop hates the governor."

"I've never whispered in my sleep or spoken aloud that I hate the governor," declared Miguel, in his usual, rasping voice.

"What a man has lost on earth he is apt to hope for in heaven," suggested Montana. He saw the blow tell, but only in the slightest lifting of the brows of his companion. "Besides," went on Montana, "your *cantina* is just at the door of his fort. How many times has he sat his horse outside your place and called for drinks for himself and his men?"

The mouth of Miguel twisted aside.

"And how many times has he paid for them?" demanded Montana. "Besides, after what has happened to you, you cannot love any of the people of authority."

"What has happened to me?" asked Miguel.

"You have been in the Valley of the Dead. You have been one of the dead in the Valley."

Miguel said nothing. He only shifted his glance sharply aside towards the girl.

"Even if everything you say should be true—and I admit nothing," said Miguel, "how could a one-legged worm like me help you to break open the fort of Duraya?"

"Yes, tell us that!" breathed the girl.

"You are the key to the fortress," said Montana, turning suddenly to Rosita.

"I?" she cried.

"How many of the jolly officers, how many of the corporals and the sergeants, would give their souls for a smile from you, Rosita?" asked Montana.

She shrugged her shoulders.

"But a girl like you," went on Montana, "will put a smile in every man's glass and let him go away with that alone. You save yourself for one of the brave and the great. A man with a carriage and six horses, gold on his uniform, and a sword at his side, and a house where Rosita can be a lady."

She turned her back on him and walked to the window, and stood with her face close to the black shimmering of the glass, though she could hardly be able to see much except her own thoughts by this light. Miguel, as he looked after her, almost smiled.

"You are the key to the castle and the fort, Rosita," said Montana. "Tell me how you will use the key. It is no army that wants to get in. Only two men. Only myself and my friend. Tell me what to do, and you will be paid."

He took out a money-belt and poured gold pieces out of it.

"This is gringo money," he said.

And he stacked little bright, five-dollar gold pieces on the table—ten stacks of ten pieces—five hundred dollars. It was not a great sum for the north of the Rio Grande. But it was almost a fortune in this part of the world.

"Do you see, Rosita?" asked Miguel.

She came slowly, sullenly back from the window. She looked at the money; she looked at Montana. Then, with a quick movement she cuffed half of the gold from the table and knocked it, clinking and spinning, across the room.

For a moment more she considered Montana with such bright malice that it seemed as though she would rush at him. Instead she whirled around and fled from the room. The door slammed behind her. Her heels clacked rapidly on the stairway.

"You have your answer," said Miguel.

"No," said Montana. "She did not run back into the *cantina*. She ran out into the open night."

He went to the door, opened it, and then returned to his chair.

"Will you sit here and wait with me till she comes back, or shall I wait alone?" asked Montana.

"Tell me how you got so much gringo gold?"

Montana thought.

"There was a gringo dog of a crooked gambler," he said. "The fellow played a very good game of cards. He could run up a pack with a crimp in it ready for me to cut. He won some money till I discovered the trick, and then I began to serve *him* with a pack that had two crimps in it. I saw the bright of his eyes when he found the first one, but he felt his way straight down to the second and made the cut without a thought of harm. Because of that, he gave me all the money in his pocket, his horse, his saddle, and some new gringo words which I learned to repeat after him."

For the first time, Miguel abandoned his reserve. He leaned forward in the enjoyment of this story. His eyes shone. And at the end he licked his lips like a beast that has been fed.

"That's good!" he repeated over and over. "That's what a man could do with two hands and ten fingers that have wits in the ends of them. Well, you can wait here alone for Rosita. Only—I give you my word that you'll have trouble with her. She can generally smile no matter what is inside her heart. When she shows herself like this, it means that she is very angry. And I, Miguel Santos, would rather have a devil angry with me than pretty little Rosita."

He got up and stumped from the room.

"Shall I sleep here?" asked Montana.

"If you dare," answered Miguel Santos. "And I'll send out a man to take care of your horse."

When he got to the door he paused and said:

"José, I believe that you are coming to steal the emeralds. I believe you want them for the bishop and not for your own pocket.   I believe that you took that gold all away from a gringo gambler.   I believe that you are a very brave and clever man.   And yet still you are a great liar!"

After that, he went out, followed by the bow which Montana had risen to give to his host.

CHAPTER XI

Now that he was perfectly alone, the Kid drew out of his pocket a small ball of very thin, hard twine. From the lower hinge of the open door he tied it across to the bottom of a chair. After that, he sat down at the table, with his back turned squarely to the door, and took up a scrap of paper on which he wrote:

"Rosita, why are you angry? Your good wishes I could never buy; but time and trouble and a little danger should be paid for. I suppose that you will send some-one now, big and proved and strong, to see whether he or I ought to be wearing this suit of yellow leather with all the silver spangles scattered over it. Besides, if he wants an extra reward after drawing the blood or the brains out of me, he can pick up the five hundred dollars from the table and the floor. By his size and his strength, I shall know how much you value me. I sit here, therefore, and pray that he may be very big. No matter how much he may frighten me, therefore—he will also make me smile——"

Something fainter than the sound of a heartbeat stirred on the stairs outside the house.

The pencil of the Kid ran on swiftly:

"But if he changes his mind about taking me away, how long will it be before you come yourself through the open door, Rosita?"

He had written to that point when he heard the noise of a caught breath, like a grunt of effort, and he whirled from the table with a gun in his hand in time to see a huge fellow with a convulsed face sprawling forward in mid-air, a knife shining in his outstretched hand. The chair was groaning forward along the floor. He must have leaped from the doorway to get at the stranger and drive the knife home surely between the shoulder-blades.

As he fell, face down on the floor, the barrel of Montana's gun rang loudly on his skull. The big man pulled up his legs and straightened them again slowly, with a shudder. Then he lay still.

Montana turned him on his back. He was no common man. Murder must have paid him very well, in times past, and he had put on a superior smile in the twist of his long moustaches, in the close fit and the brilliant braid of his jacket, and the crimson silk of the sash which he wore around his waist. There was only a dash too much of the brute in his face. Otherwise he was a good-looking fellow. And he was big enough to have stepped on a horse as another man might step on a pony.

He had a good, new revolver as well as the knife. Montana took the weapons. Also he took a pin used at the throat of the man's shirt, because it was garnished with two big rubies. By this time the Mexican had begun to stir. In half a second he roused from complete oblivion to cat-quick life, and leaped to his feet.

"Sit down, friend," said the Kid. "Rosita will want to see what you've done."

"Witchcraft!" said the stranger, with one hand on his bumped head and the other at his throat.

"Not witchcraft. Only a piece of string," said Montana. "There it is, from the door to the chair. What's your name?"

"Benito Garza," said the big man.

"Untie the string and put it on the table; but don't try to bolt through the door. Because there's a real witchcraft inside this gun of mine."

Benito Garza, with a stupefied face, obediently untied the string and brought it to the table. He stood back against the wall, lifting his hand to his face. A trickle of blood ran down from a great bruise over one eye. The eye itself began to swell, redden, close.

"Sit down," said Montana.

Garza sank into a chair, keeping his grip on the side of it with one hand as though to prevent a second magical fall.

"How long have you known Rosita?" asked the Kid.

"May the devil——" began Garza.

"Hush!" said the Kid, and Garza was hushed.

"How long have you known Rosita?"

"A year—two years—how can I tell? It isn't the time that counts in the knowing of a girl."

"That's true," answered Montana. "But you can see that she told you the truth. There's the gold on the table. You can see some more of it on the floor."

"She told you what she would tell me?" queried Benito Garza.

"Not a word. But she had a look in her eye when she left me. Sit quietly, there. Be patient, Benito, and you'll see her again before long, I think."

Benito sat motionless. Now and then he raised his hand and smeared the blood on his face without stopping the small flow of it. Some of the red ran down into his moustaches and soaked and made half of the fine spring of them droop down, and blood still ran from the bedraggled tip and splashed unheeded on the tight trousers leg of Garza.

But the Kid was smoking his second cigarette before the girl appeared in the open doorway. Her eyes were wide and blank with a vague seeing, like that of a sleepwalker, or the vision of second sight.

"Here is Benito. I kept him so that you could see that he is not very much hurt," said the Kid.

She made no answer. Garza did not exist in her eyes.

"Now that she's here again," said Montana, "you can take your knife and gun from the table, Garza, and leave us. *Adios*. Good fortune on the road and with the señoritas."

Garza, picking up his weapons, swayed for an instant in hesitant indecision. All his nature must have been urging him to renew the fight which had been ended almost as it began. Perhaps it was the shock to his head and the more fatal blow to his vanity that made him turn with lowered head and leave the room, and pass, stumbling, down the stairs outside.

And still the girl was staring.

"Come a little closer," said Montana. "Benito Garza is a gallant sort of a fellow, after all. He wouldn't leave without making some little offering to you, Rosita. And here's a pin with two good rubies on it. It will hold that rose in your hair. You see? Like this. Now look at yourself in the mirror!"

As he stepped back from her, smiling, she exclaimed in a whisper:

"El Keed!"

The name hit him hard. It had been hunted too many hundreds, too many thousands, of miles through Old Mexico. Perhaps there was a bit of cold fear in his eyes as comprehension came slowly into those of the girl.

"Now I remember it!" she said. "It was a hot afternoon. There were twenty men drinking in the garden. You sat in the corner, alone. Now I remember everything. You were all Mexican except the blue of your eyes and something about your smiling."

"I've learned more about that, now, and so have you, Rosita. You used to show more of your teeth when you smiled."

She took a breath.

"El Keed!" she whispered again, and cast a sudden glance over her shoulder at the open door, as though the name must have issued on wings from the room to fly through the town and make men reach for hats and weapons. "Mother of heaven, why have you come here again?"

"For the good bishop and for you, Rosita."

"Hush!"

"Well," said El Keed, "you tell me the truth about myself, then?"

"To go like a devil with wings and find trouble!"

"There is plenty of trouble in you—and in the emerald crown, Rosita. I swore that no one would recognize me with such a dark skin. Besides, it has been a long time since I was in Duraya."

"I looked at your mare in the stable. She was too beautiful for any *charro* to ride. When I looked at the lantern-light sleeking over her skin I knew that no common man could have ridden her into Duraya, and I ran out to call back that poor Benito. But he was already in the room. I waited to hear noise. There was no noise. My heart stopped. I began to ask myself who you were. I began to half-remember. And you are El Keed!"

She was backing towards the door.

"Why do you sneak away?" asked Montana. "Call out! Sing out my name, and there are twenty men downstairs who'll come fast enough, with your father among 'em. If he knew, he's good enough Mexican to help cut my throat!"

"That is true. And he must not know."

"Why did you send Benito Garza?"

"Why did you try to buy me like a dog?"

"Because you need plenty of money. With this much you could be a lady with a *duenna* in Mexico City."

She tossed back her head and caught her breath.

"But this is a game, El Keed, and everyone who plays a game with you is sure to lose."

"Until I lose my head," said Montana.

"In the fort of Duraya?"

"Or here in this *cantina*. I'm losing it now, Rosita."

"Look at me, El Keed."

"I'm looking, Rosita."

"I am a pretty girl, am I not?"

"I've been remembering you all this time, but remembering was no good."

"But look, El Keed. I'm not too tall and not too short. I shall never be heavy. I shall never let fat swallow up my face. I'll fight fat like fire."

"You'll always be lovely, Rosita."

"I can dance and sing. Also, I can talk almost like a lady. Some day you may see."

"You can talk like an angel, Rosita."

"To be pretty is to work very hard and to keep smiling," said the girl.

"Of course it is. But you've stopped smiling, Rosita."

"I'll never smile for you," said she. "Oh, I could look at you and let my heart jump out at my eyes. But how long would you keep it?"

"For ever," said Montana.

"Bah! Your for ever is a day or a week or a month. And then you would grow tired because you have to ride. There is always the other side of the mountain to see. And what girl could ride fast enough to keep up with you?"

She closed her eyes.

"El Keed!"

"Ay?" said Montana.

"Kiss me and tell me to forget everything I've said."

He leaned over her until she could feel the shadow of his face.

"No, *compañera*," said he.

CHAPTER XII

MONTANA, the next morning, sat at the table in his room and saw a peon carry in a tray loaded with savoury roast kid such as Mexico alone can offer. There were tortillas, frijoles cooked with seven kinds of peppers, green and yellow and red. And a good red wine, also, to wash everything down. When he had eaten, Rosita appeared in the door.

"Was everything to the pleasure of the señor?" she asked.

He took up his guitar and rose from the table. He strummed the tight strings softly with the flat of his fingers, a breathing accompaniment hardly larger than a whisper, and the voice in which he sang could not have escaped even through an open window of the room.

Perhaps there is no other Spanish song much older than that which he sang to her:

> "*Love is not happiness.*
> *A horse under heel ;*
> *A sword under hand ;*
> *And red wine for the belly ;*
> *But love is not happiness.*"

The girl leaned her hand against the edge of the door and listened with a bowed head.

He went on:

"*Love is not happiness.*
Seeing is longing ;
Winning is doubting ;
Leaving is sorrow ;
But love is not happiness."

"You know the old songs," said the girl.

"I love the old songs," said the Kid.

"You have old ways, also," said the girl, "and a few new ones."

"Are you sad, Rosita?"

"Is there one more man in the world like El Keed?"

"I hope not, poor fellow," said he.

"If I met one more like you, I should go mad."

"Think of this, Rosita. You are heart-whole and free. You are going to open for me, this evening, a door into the fort of Duraya. That's a good deed, considering what I shall try to do when I'm inside. And afterwards you'll have the five hundred dollars with which you can take five hundred steps among the grandees in Mexico City. Five hundred steps? You would hardly have to take five before you walked yourself into a carriage belonging to a governor at least. That is why I know I shall have to ride a long trail to see you again, if I live to come out of Duraya. I may have to ride as far as Paris. Would you know me, there?"

"That is what I keep saying and never believing. I've taken the money. I *have* been bought."

"Only for a good deed, Rosita."

"Do you mean that you would ride after me—if everything goes happily?"

"To the end of the world."

"But just now you would not have to ride. You would only need to walk three steps."

"And leave the emerald crown in the hands of that General Estrada?"

She lifted her head, finally, and gave him a long, long look behind which he could read, with a perfect understanding, that many devious thoughts were working through her mind.

"Well," she said, suddenly picking up the tray, "I've sent the messenger to your friend. If he comes up the back stairs, no one worth while will see him. This evening, if you knock as I told you on the small door, it will be opened. And then—God defend you!"

She went out like that, suddenly; and the Kid stared for a long moment at the door which had closed behind her.

After that, he picked up the guitar and began to sing again, almost soundlessly, the love songs of old Spain, and Mexico, all of them sad. But, afterwards, he stood for a long time in front of a window, looking out and up at the great, squat walls of the fort of Duraya. Somewhere a bugle was blowing thin and small, and he could always see the sentries walking their posts on the walls. It was true that General Estrada was a warrior who knew his business in the world very well. If he had been given a province already picked bare as a stone, he had made up for that by robbing a church. And inside his fort one could be sure that all was working in perfect order, as a military machine ought to be.

It was a little later in the day when bare feet shuffled on the back stairs, followed by the soft clacking of loosely bound *huaraches*. Then Rubriz came through the door, barefooted, with a huge sombrero of tattered straw on his head and the moustaches shaved from his face. Even the scar had been covered by an unfading dye, and his lips bulged out in a way that distorted the entire expression of his face.

The towering bulk of Brother Pascual entered behind the outlaw. And Rubriz, throwing himself down in a chair, first plucked out of his mouth the rubber wadding which helped to disguise his face. Then he sighed:

"You've sent for us, Montana. Here we are. There is the fort. And neither Pascual nor I as yet one step closer to an idea or a key that will open the place and give us a way to the emeralds. And here you lie at your soft ease, like a puma asleep after a kill, till the dogs get wind of you and run you to bay. Is that wine in that bottle?"

He made inquiry with his nose and then poured the contents of the bottle, uninvited, down his throat. After that he made and lighted a cigarette. Pascual, in the meantime, stood ill at ease in a shadowy corner of the room.

"We need," said Montana, "a man to hold our horses in the right place. Pascual will do it for us. We also need 'soup.' Have some dynamite boiled down during the day, Mateo. Get the fuse and the rest we'll need to blow a safe, and some yellow soap to run a mould."

"What safe?" asked the bandit.

"Up in the tower is the room of the governor, with his office in front of it. And in a corner of the room there is an old safe, but a strong one."

"Are the emeralds in that safe?" asked Rubriz.

"How can I tell? But if they're not in that safe, where would they be, friend?"

"Very well. That is one thing learned. What else?"

"Here is a plan of the inside of the fort. Every room and every gallery is marked down. And all the courts. And the sentry posts are marked in red, you see?"

"I see," said Rubriz, poring over the plan. "All that we need, now, is a pair of wings to fly over the walls, unless the sentries are ready to shoot us out of the air."

"Come to meet me, to-night, just after dark, at this same place. Or wait here the rest of the day with me," said Montana. "Pascual can get the horses, in the meantime. He can keep them down in the willows by the bank of the river. You know where the willows are thickest, down there, Pascual?"

"I know," agreed the friar.

"Ay, but how to get into the fort?" demanded Rubriz.

"That will be managed. I know a certain way to tap on a certain postern down at the bottom of the wall above the river. And my tap will bring out a certain sergeant with a smile on his face and his hands empty. If he leaves the door open behind him, can we trust ourselves to get inside, *amigo*?"

Rubriz began to sweat. His face shone almost as brightly as his eyes.

"What lies inside the door?" he asked.

"A guardroom with two private soldiers inside."

"And these two?"

"There are only two of them, Mateo."

"Ay, but two can alarm ten thousand."

"There was never any good plan without a little risk in it," answered El Keed, shrugging his shoulders.

"Look!" muttered Rubriz to Pascual. "He is a devil, eh?"

"He does a work in the name of a kind God," said the friar, devoutly.

"And how do you know that the fool of a sergeant will open the door when you tap?"

"He is not a fool. He's only a man in love."

"Hai, brother! And you know the girl a little better than he knows her?"

"Five hundred dollars' worth better. That's all."

"It's a good bit of difference."

"He's told her that if she ever comes to that postern and raps on it in a certain rhythm, he'll be out instantly, and have her in his arms. If he should put his hands on Mateo Rubriz, instead, that would be only his hard luck, I'd say!"

CHAPTER XIII

Down among the willows the light thickened earlier and there was a tone of green added to the gloom. Here, as the day ended with its sudden fires in the sky, Rubriz and Montana met the big friar. Brother Pascual was gravely and deeply excited. He led his own mule, the great black stallion of Rubriz, and that red-silk beauty, the mare of the Kid. As the darkness seemed to lift in a wave that closed at last over the walls of Fort Duraya, the friar said:

"If I could go with you, friends, it seems to me that I should be happier than any other man in the world."

"Three men can be seen where two might slip by," answered Montana. "And knowing that you're out here, waiting, will make us that much stronger if we ever get inside the fort."

"Wait for us till the morning," said Rubriz. "Then wait again to-morrow evening. If we have not come by that midnight, go your way and forget us. Give my stallion to the bishop, if he's brave enough to ride the black horse."

"And take the red mare," said Montana, "a good two days' march into the mountains. When you come to grass and water, and no man's house in sight, turn her loose without a strap on her back."

"I shall do it," said the friar. "I swear under the eye of Heaven. Brothers, give me your hands."

They were given to him, and he exclaimed in his great, deep voice:

"We three are bound together. The warmth of our blood commingles and the breath of one spirit moves in us. There is more than the strength of earth in us. Bishop Emiliano prays for you to-night. Be strong. Be patient. And I shall wait here and pray in my turn. If only I could fill my hands in this work, instead of filling my throat with words!"

When the honest friar had finished speaking, the quick dark of the night already had closed over the town, and Montana and Rubriz went up the slope towards the fort through the first blackness. As they climbed the slope they could hear the voices from the town, the singing, the barking of dogs, the slamming of doors, the shrilling of children still playing through the dim shafts of the lamplight, and here and there men laughing, men in anger, shouting. But all of these sounds of life drifted up to them gradually, like water rising in a well.

They were close to the black and rigid heights of the fort wall when they paused, out of a common impulse, and looked behind them. All the stars were shining except towards the east and south, where thick clouds had unfurled close to the horizon. Perhaps a storm was moving up from that direction. But all was placid and the night was so windless near by that they could see the thin faces of the stars in the shallows of the river loop near the willows where the good Brother Pascual was waiting for them.

"Now, I tell you this," said Rubriz, softening his mighty voice to secrecy. "It is better to have the naked prayers of a fellow like that Pascual than a hundred strong men at your back, all with arms in their hands."

After that he turned briskly about and went straight

on, with Montana, towards the little postern which was let into the lower wall of the fort. They could mark the place, from a distance, by the ragged line of light which sketched in the cracks of the doorway.

When they were standing before it, Montana lifted his hand. Rubriz at once stepped up against the wall, flattening himself against it. There he waited while Montana rapped twice, paused, rapped twice again, and then three times, rapidly and lightly.

There was only a moment's pause, and then a key was heard turning. Great bolts slid back, one by one, each making a light clanking sound as it disengaged; and finally the heavy door began to sag outwards. As it opened, voices thrust out into the night.

"Be tender, Andres."

"Be kind, Andres!"

"Be still, you fools!" panted a quick, harsh answer from close to the door.

It yawned wider, until the lamplight was glistening over the thick iron plates which shod the inside of the postern, studded with the heads of a hundred rivets big enough to have been worked into the side of the mightiest of liners.

He who was thrusting the door open could be seen at the same time, one of those men who are big from the waist up and bowlegged beneath, the legs bending as though to support and balance more easily the top-heavy bulk above. He wore wrinkled cotton trousers and *huaraches*, but above the waist, where his body became more important, his uniform grew splendid, also, and wound up in epauletted shoulders fit to have graced a major, at the least. He wore at his belt a long sheathed knife and a revolver, and he carried a rifle slung over his shoulder, for that was the constant rule with all the men of that wary old fox, General Estrada.

"Señorita—Rosita—my dear!" whispered the panting voice of the sergeant as he thrust himself at last through the gap of the opening door into the dark of the night outside. "Where are you, my sacred beauty?"

The blow that fell on him made a dull sound, because it struck on the padding of muscles just over the juncture of head and neck. Even then, only the extraordinary flesh of Sergeant Andres prevented him from sustaining a fracture of the spinal column or the neck vertebræ, because Rubriz had struck from the side and with much enthusiasm.

Montana, gliding forward from the opposite side, received the toppling weight in his arms and laid it in a heap upon the ground.

"Well, close the door, at least," said a voice inside the door, "or we'll have to come and look out, Andres!"

"We've counted to ten, and the door is still not closed. Poor Andres, is this our fault or yours?"

The two began to laugh.

"Let me go first!" said one.

"Keep back, you fool! I've started already."

They came, scuffling, and struck their shoulders against the door, which shuddered open with a slight groaning of the hinges. Into the widening shaft of light which was allowed to escape into the night in this manner, stepped the masked face of Montana, with Rubriz scarcely behind him.

Their levelled revolvers drove the soldiers back in a confusion. But they did not actually flee. Rubriz was cursing them by all the names of his favourite saints.

"Run, you rats! Run, dog-stealers! Run, brindled swine—and give me a chance to jump on you behind and pull back your heads to cut your throats the better! Ay, run, fools! Don't stand waiting!"

But they could not run. The husky sobbing of his

breath paralysed them, for he seemed like a man already drinking blood.

Montana, unaided, lifted up the bulk of the fallen sergeant, dragged him inside the door, and let his loosened weight spill down on the floor. Staring at him as he pulled the door shut again to keep in the tell-tale, broadening arm of light that advanced into the darkness, Montana thought that the man was actually dead. There was a faint froth on his lips, that no longer bubbled. His face had blackened a trifle. His eyes were only partially opened. But at this moment he uttered a snoring sound from the deep bottom of his throat.

Montana stepped over him and saw that Rubriz had turned his men against the wall and had taken away their weapons. He was rapidly tying their wrists together.

One of the soldiers was only a boy. The frightful threats of the masked outlaw had drained away all his strength. He began to weep in a small, weak voice, getting out the name of a saint or of Heaven every now and then.

"Soldiers? I could make a better soldier out of wet cornmeal!" said Rubriz. "O God! *amigo*, when I see such men as these in the uniforms of soldiers."

"Ay," said the dry-eyed member of the pair. "Curse him, the poor dog! But I am Porfirio Oros! I am a known man! Let me have an equal chance with either of you, and I'll fight like two men. I am Porfirio Oros. I am ready to die like a man!"

He began to make his voice louder, as the ecstasy came over him. He was a little lump of a fat man, who looked as soft as butter.

"Gag 'em," said Montana, and set to work on the fat man first.

The second soldier began to scream. He got out one half-breath of sound before Rubriz beat out the voice with a stroke of his fist and then began to thrust a wadded piece of cloth between the teeth of the guard.

"Not too deep and not too hard," cautioned Montana. "We don't want to have dead men behind us, *amigo*."

"Will you tell me how to gag a man?" exclaimed Rubriz angrily. "Remember, *amigo*, that I was gagging men while you were still in the cradle, and I have gagged them ever since. If any man in the world has the touch, I am he. I have gagged men with the finest in Mexico, and not one in ten has died afterwards. A man I have gagged lives to be a wiser and a milder fellow. Gagging, friend, makes a man fond of quiet talk, or no talk at all, the rest of his days."

He finished trussing his man as he spoke. They turned to the sergeant. He was barely breathing. And because of that, Montana took charge of the gagging, making sure that the wad of cloth was worked well inside the mouth, but that the tongue was not thrust back into the throat, with a chance of strangling poor Andres.

Now three soldiers of General Estrada lay on their faces, side by side, each tied to the other, so that movement would be impossible for all.

"How much time has that cost us?" muttered Rubriz.

"You've promised me," answered the Kid. "No murder, Mateo!"

"Call it what you want," said Rubriz, "but the kind God who watches us knows how much time we've wasted here in His honour, when we might have left them still for ever, with a thrust apiece. Come on, *amigo*. I know the way. I've memorized every turn of every hall in the place!"

He went on, leading straight up a flight of stairs which was drilled through the thickness of the great old walls of the fort of Duraya.

Behind them, all the three men lay still, but the sergeant was beginning to move his jaws a little. He stirred them with care, and he began to push with his tongue against the base of the wadding that kept him from drawing a free breath.

After a time his tongue seemed to swell with the efforts he had been making. His throat appeared to be closing, also. He had to struggle to get any breath into his lungs.

Then he could not breathe at all.

With this, in a frightful panic, he heaved himself to his knees so strongly that the other two were dragged out of place, also. He tugged with all his might. The twine that bound his wrists cut through the skin like dull blades of knives. But every effort he made only stifled him the more.

This he realized.

There were two pairs of hands besides his own, ready with a gesture to pluck the strangling thing from his mouth, but all those hands were helpless as his own.

The sergeant remembered an old-folk tale out of his youth. And suddenly he saw that to struggle was to kill himself. If he were to make headway of any kind, he would have to relax himself in every muscle first. Then he might be able to breathe.

So he dropped down. His face was in the dust, but this did not matter.

He could feel the pressure of the blood thrusting up in his cheeks. His neck was swelling. Even to open his eyes was difficult.

He began to think of death, but as he visualized it, and as he determined that he would beat out his brains against the rock to shorten the agony, he suddenly discovered that a needle of coldness was thrusting into the fever of his throat.

And then he realized that it was a whiff of air. It drew in audibly through the horrible slaver that filled his mouth. His whole throat was growing cooler.

And presently he knew that his life was saved. And he could actually breathe. By degrees he was going to reduce the burning agony of fire in his lungs.

Instead of pausing to thank God for this deliverance, with the stubbornness of a hero, or of a brute, he instantly commenced making fresh efforts to work the gag from his mouth.

CHAPTER XIV

THE map of the fort which the Kid had been able to draw out of the information of Miguel Santos and the girl seemed perfectly accurate, and as Rubriz had boasted, it was perfectly in his mind. He led the way without a flaw up the two flights of stairs which had been cut into the wall of the fortress and then into a great hall, long and narrow, where only two or three weak lights were burning. Three long tables ran down the centre of the room. On the walls hung flags that represented all of the regiments which had ever served in the garrison of Duraya. In the farther corner of this hall was a door which opened upon a short corridor that ran directly to the tower apartments of General Ignacio Estrada, in command. The two were not quite across the floor when hinges creaked. Montana, leaping into the black of the corner, whirled to see that a dozen young officers had entered the room, carrying a big hamper, and that Rubriz was still visible to them. His bare foot had slipped on a stone as he strove to spring after Montana.

And at that instant a bawling voice cried:

"Mozo! Hai! Come here and pick up this hamper. What are gentlemen to do? Wait on themselves when there are dogs like you around?"

"Stand fast! Don't move for me!" gasped Rubriz to the Kid, covertly tearing away his mask as he spoke. "Pray for me! I front them!"

And he turned and walked straight back towards the group!

"Run!" shouted one of the officers.

And Rubriz obediently ran, springing forward with wonderful lightness in spite of the bulk of his unwieldy body.

"The basket on the table. Stand away, Pedro, and let this fellow do the work."

"He can't lift it," said Pedro.

"Can't he, though? Look at the shoulders of him. If they're not all fat, he may be able to. These poor devils have strength."

There was a sudden shout as Rubriz leaned, lifted the basket, and slid it on to the table.

"That's Mexico!" said the oldest of the officers. "Look at the muscles in those legs! Pull off your dirty shirt and let's see your body, too!"

"Forgive me," panted Rubriz. "I am called to my work. Another——"

"Hai! Are you working for soldiers and question commands? Show him the way, Pedro! Off with it!"

Two of them grabbed the cheap white shirt and instantly it was ripped from the back of Rubriz.

"There!" called out the commander. "Did I tell you? Not fat, either. All muscle—all pure strength. I'd stake that man against a mule. Where did you get those leg muscles, man?"

"In the mines, sir," said Rubriz, his head bowed, his shaggy hair falling forward.

"Look at him! He's ashamed to be naked, even before men. What are those white marks? Scars? Knife cuts? Come on, and we'll find a story in this one. Open the wine!"

That was quickly done. The hamper was thickly packed with wine-bottles, and the corks had barely ceased popping before glasses began to brim and pour down wide throats.

The Kid, from his corner, covered the gay little party with two revolvers and shifted his aim from breast to breast, from head to head. He was perfectly convinced, now, that he and Rubriz could never escape from the fort. But if they died, so would some of these jolly sparks.

"What are these scars? What sort of a mozo are you?" asked the commander. "More like a damned mountain bandit, to my eye. Look at him and try to remember! Haven't I seen that face on posters with a reward for him, dead or alive?"

The nerves of Montana prickled through his skin. It seemed that the next moment would be the end of Rubriz, or the beginning of the end.

But the deep voice of the outlaw answered:

"I was hurt by a fall in the mine, sirs. I was carrying a basket up the ladder——"

"And the damned ladder broke and gave you a fall?" asked the commander.

He leaned back a little, his thin face sneering as he stared at the half-naked, powerful body of Mateo Rubriz.

"No, but the forehead band that supported the basket of ore broke, and the basket fell and knocked another man off the ladder. That man was killed by his fall."

"Listen! I told you there were stories in this lump of a man."

"I was only a few steps from the top of the ladder and, as I came up, the overseer, who had seen what had happened, hit me with the butt of his man-whip, and that knocked me down into the shaft again."

"You see how they treat these fellows? The other man was killed, but you lived through it, eh?"

"I was weeks in the hospital," said Rubriz.

"Discipline," declared the officer. "That's what it makes. Knock fools over the head when they make mistakes, and there'll be fewer mistakes."

"There'll be more broken heads," said Pedro.

"What do you mean? Look at this head! It would still take a parcel of breaking. Not many brains under that shock of hair, but enough to know how to lift hampers of wine for his betters. And for all that he's been through, he still has a light enough foot and hand—a light enough hand to steal the gold out of your teeth while you sleep, I'll wager. Jump up there on the table and give us a dance, you!"

"There is no music, sir," said Rubriz.

The officer picked up a quirt, drew the lashes through his hand, and then struck the table.

"Up on the table, and we'll give you music!" he shouted. "Up with you!"

And he slashed Rubriz across the naked body.

It seemed to Montana, as his thumbs hooked over the hammers of the revolvers, ready to open fire, that Rubriz swayed in the very act of hurling himself at the man of the whip. Instead, without touching the table with his hands, he leaped lightly on top of it. The officers shouted. They began to strike the table in a quick rhythm with their whips. And to that rhythm poor Rubriz had to dance. When some of them made a mistake and landed heavily on his body instead of on the table, he had to leap the higher.

It was frantic work. In a few minutes he was staggering. And at last Pedro it was who called out:

"Let the poor fool stop. See, Luis, where you drew the blood on him! He's had enough exercise for one evening. Get down, mozo."

Rubriz jumped to the floor.

"Give him a few coppers," said Pedro, "and he'll be able to forget his torn shirt."

"What about his torn skin?"

"What does skin matter? It grows again without any cost!"

There was a sudden shout of applause for this.

"Here, give him some wine!"

"Don't be a fool. He'd rather have pulque."

"Here's the money."

"It's too much," decided thin-faced Luis, the superior officer, and he dropped a portion of it, calmly, into his own pocket.

"Give him the rest, then," said Pedro.

"Give it to him? Give a dog food with my own hand? Let him root for it, the swine!"

So Luis hurled the money from him. It rattled on the floor. It rolled clinking into the farthest corners, and Rubriz darted after it, sometimes almost skidding on hands and knees in his apparent eagerness. The officers followed his antics with yells of the highest appreciation. But a toast proposed by one of them suddenly called all heads and all eyes towards their own group. It was at that moment that Montana drew open the door into the corridor of the general rooms and big Rubriz sprang through the gap.

His eyes were insane. There was only one guttering light here, in the foul air, by which to see the outlaw, but even that light was too much for Montana. Rubriz, for an instant, buried his hands in his hair. Then he turned and beat his head against the wall.

Only for a long moment could he hold up one hand. When he opened it Montana could see a dozen copper coins in the palm.

"Eleven!" gasped Rubriz. "Eleven men in the uniforms of officers—by fire, Montana! No, by the whip! By the whip! And you—you stood in the corner, gringo, and laughed as they beat me—as Rubriz danced for them! O God!—I—Mateo Rubriz! You laughed! Eleven in uniforms—eleven at once! I shall have them—and listen to them screaming as the whips cut closer to the bones! Ha, Montana, kill me! I can't live! To breathe for ten minutes more is too much torture! I am going back to kill them now."

"Kill one or two and be flogged to death by the rest?" asked the Kid. "I thought you were talking about revenge?"

Rubriz wiped his mouth on the back of his hairy arm. So, gasping for his breath, he drew himself back little by little towards calm. The Kid stood with his back turned on the ugly picture.

Afterwards he heard a murmuring voice behind him:

"You could have killed a few of them. I would have helped with the rest. Instead, San Juan of Capistrano, fix the day when I can put my hands on this gringo. Now we work together, but afterwards there will be a day!"

"Are you finished?" asked Montana, calmly, over his shoulder.

Rubriz bit at the air like a dog, as though this last reproof cut deeper than all that had passed before. But he spoke quietly when he answered:

"I am finished—for this night, gringo!"

And stepping past Montana, he actually took the lead along the damp little corridor to the small door at the farther end. The soot from the lamp had half-poisoned the air; the foul sweet of it was in the nostrils of Montana until he had to fight to keep from sneezing.

Rubriz, pushing the door open the slightest crack, pressed his ear close to the crevice in order to listen. After a long moment he widened the fissure; he stepped right out in the apartments of General Ignacio Estrada. And not a living soul was in them!

It seemed to Montana, as the greatness of the relief poured over him like a soothing stream of warm water, that there had been a payment made through the sufferings and the terrible shame of Rubriz, and that now all would go smoothly forward until they had escaped with the prize they sought.

The glimmering light of two lamps that showed them the comfort of the rooms was to him an assurance and a promise.

CHAPTER XV

THE governor had done his best. Of course his predecessor had cleared out the "palace" corner of the fort to the last stick of furniture when he removed from the post. There had not been time for Estrada to refurnish all the lower stories of the palace, but he had fitted up his private rooms at the top according to his personal ideas of luxury.

Hanging things pleased General Estrada. He had hanging lamps set about with the crystals of chandeliers. Heavy red drapes of velvet separated his bedroom from his study. Two-fold curtains swept over the high faces of the casements. And the four-poster bed was all garlanded about, as it were, with rosy and golden stuffs that might have brightened a bridal suite. There were other details that made Rubriz scowl and Montana smile; above all, there was the chair of audience in the general's study, which was in fact like a throne, complete with a cushioned footstool for his big feet.

Rubriz locked the door and then went to the throne, where he sat down. His gross brown body, naked to the waist, lolled on a velvet-lined arm of the chair; his bare toes wriggled into the softness of the footstool.

"To tie him in this chair," murmured Rubriz, "and then to bring his eleven officers and to tie them up by their thumbs to that rafter, and to put fires under their feet, and to burn 'em one by one and let this Estrada keep tasting death for hours before he died—do you see what a beautiful thing that could be, *amigo?* "

The study of the general was also used, apparently, as a private dining-room from time to time. At any rate, there was a square table, and a sideboard on which appeared a fantastic lot of rococo silver, none of the pieces mating the rest, but all huge, ponderous, worth less than the weight of the metal in them. The door of a cabinet was open, and liqueurs of many colours gleamed from the bottles inside.

"But the safe! The safe!" exclaimed Rubriz. "All the information is perfect except the one important thing. Here I sit like a king—a naked king—and still we've not found the safe!"

They went back into the bedroom again. They swayed the curtains here and there, vainly. Montana had given up hope when Rubriz pulled open a door and uttered a faint, moaning cry of joy. It was a huge closet, large enough to be called a room, and it held only one thing, the tall face of a safe, painted black and yellow.

"It is here!" said Rubriz. "And we have the emerald crown, and then some angel or devil will show us how to get out of this place and back through the postern after we've blown the safe door off its hinges. To work, *amigo*! Thank God that you were carrying the 'soup.' And still, if I had had it, I might have been able to throw it under the feet of eleven officers. If the explosion carried me to hell with them, I should have laughed all the way."

In fact, the position was perfect, so that if the explosion took place, the closet would confine part of the noise, and the greater part of it; the rest might be muffled away by the ponderous walls and the strong floors of the "castle."

But before Montana could set to work to run the mould around the safe, a hand began to beat on the door of the governor's outer room. Very clearly Montana could hear a voice bellowing:

"Excellency! Open the door! It is Sergeant Andres! Thieves have entered the fort—thieves or murderers! They have come in through the postern!"

"Bind softly—be easy with the gags!" said Rubriz, bitterly, to the Kid. "Now we are dead men! Why did I ever trust a gringo? You are all women!"

It seemed the end to Montana, and as he drew his guns he stared at the savage body and face of big Rubriz, and at the foolish luxury of the Governor's rooms, and thought that he could have found a better place to die in.

There were many men with Sergeant Andres. They began to shake the knob of the door.

"Beat it down!" cried one of the lot. "Beat down the door! They have murdered the governor!"

Heavy shocks began to fall against the door. Booming noises echoed through the rooms, with the loud, quick shuddering of the door against its hinges, in between. There was a noise of cracking, splintering wood, but still the heavy panels of the door were holding. And far away other sounds of running footfalls, shouting voices, streamed towards the tower from all parts of the castle.

"There are the windows," said Montana.

"Ay, if we had wings," said Rubriz.

Montana sprang into the nearest casement. Below him, the wall dropped a giddy height. There were no stars. A moon was up, but it only lighted the swirling confusion of the storm clouds which had spread out of the east until almost the entire sky was covered. Gusty, warm breaths of the coming storm struck into the face of the Kid.

He dropped to his knees and peered into the dimness

below him. Then the hand of Rubriz fell on his shoulder.

"This is a thing I have always known," said the outlaw—"that one day I should be in such a place, with no escape, and the enemy all before me, and behind me a cliff that could not be climbed. Well, San Juan of Capistrano has been my friend, but now he is tired, perhaps. *Amigo*, let us be ready to die together, like men. Let us pile up the dead!"

"Look!" said Montana. "There is a ledge here, under the window. It is wide enough for a man to lie on—if the man uses care—it is almost a foot wide— it is more than a foot wide—you see?"

"Misery of my soul!" breathed the bandit, peering down through the darkness beside his friend. "Lie there? Even a bird with wings would be afraid to lie there."

"It has to be this way, or are we to surrender to bad luck, Mateo? I'll show you the way!"

As he slid through the window, the first gust of the rain struck him. The big, wind-swept drops drove through his clothing instantly to the skin, and made him tremble. Then his feet found the ledge. It was a yard and a half below the window and consisted merely of the space left where the wall receded in one of its set- backs, of which there were several between the bottom and the top.

"Follow me, Mateo!" he called. "It is possible to stand on it. Let yourself down. Stand with your toes on the outside of the ledge to slant your body in against the wall. And then——"

He could not speak again, for the outer door to the rooms of the governor now went down with a prodigious crash. He saw Mateo's bulky form swing down from the window. Then the Mexican was beside him, edging in pursuit as he worked his way cautiously along the narrow ledge.

Overhead, there was thundering of footfalls. A light swung out from the window almost instantly and disappeared again. It flashed from another window around the corner of the tower, a radiance that glittered for a moment through the slant lines of the falling rain. And then the wind came in a billow and with a booming sound and began to pry at Montana to loosen him from his hold.

He came to the corner of the tower. And here the ledge disappeared. It did not turn on to the other side of the wall. So that they were utterly checked and held, here, to a standstill.

But Mateo was cheerful, beside him.

"I was wrong!" said Rubriz. "That saint of Capistrano, that fellow is not one to lose heart. He will make this as wide as a road to us and——"

Here the voice went out of him. The wind, screaming suddenly, staggered Rubriz so that he fought for his balance with swinging arms on the verge of the foothold. And Montana, digging his feet strongly in on the edge of the rock, getting a partial handhold on the corner masonry of the tower, reached out with his left hand and pulled at the big Mexican.

The pull and the jar of the wind swung him sidewise so that the storm could get at him more fully. His left foot slipped from its purchase. He waited for the next gust to tear him loose. But as it had come suddenly, so the wind eased for a moment, while the handhold of Montana still held good.

He regained his former position, with Rubriz now desperately flattened against the wall, his arms spread out.

"Mother of Heaven! Mother of Heaven! Kind

San Juan—remember me!" gasped Rubriz. "I am no longer bad. I am only a poor, fat, foolish old man. If I must die, let me at least have my hands in the throat of another man. Gentle San Juan, do not let Rubriz die in the company of a gringo, only!"

But he followed that naïve prayer by saying, instantly: "No other man in the world would have risked himself to grab at me then!"

"It must have been your saint who made me do it," answered the Kid. And he chuckled a little, till the violence of the wind and the rushing of the rain filled his eyes and his throat.

"Death of my soul!" he heard Rubriz saying. "He laughs!"

CHAPTER XVI

THE general had come like a whirlwind as soon as the alarm reached him, and with him poured in the eleven young officers who had been drinking in their mess-hall. Others—officers, house mozos, private soldiers—formed a solid pack with the general, but he rushed through them and ran straight to the closet in which his safe was standing. There he slammed the door in the faces of the rest.

Speechless, awful fear worked in his throat. He could hardly fit the key into the old lock. But at last the heavy door swung wide and made a little moaning sound that shot despair through the heart of Ignacio Estrada.

He pulled open the one drawer that really mattered, and there he found, by the blind grasp of his hands, the treasure. Only when his hands had closed on it was he able to look. And now he saw it again, clearly, the semi-circle which had broken when he tore it from its place with the eyes of the brown image looking up towards him in resignation and in pain.

The general crowded the treasure back into its chamois bag. With the door of the safe still open, he remained on his knees for a moment, allowing the sickness to pass from his heart, while his attitude was that of one in prayer.

He had been a fool to keep the emeralds so long, bargaining with the "fences" who were willing to receive the stolen goods at a certain price. After all, they were only natural in wishing to make their profit.

Finally, he was able to get to his feet, close and lock the old safe. It was madness, he thought, to keep such valuables in such an antiquated place of safe-keeping! That would be his first step—to demand a modern safe, to preserve safely the pay of the soldiers which had to pass through his hands.

When he had come to these conclusions he took two or three deep breaths and then rubbed the colour into his swarthy cheeks and gave a few turns to his moustaches.

He was an impressive, not a handsome man. His face was built in three steps, of which the topmost stage, the forehead, was by far the briefest. It was so low and receding that he had to be continually passing his hand across his hair to keep the stiff brush of it from jagging down over his eyes.

The second stage of that pyramidal face began at the top of the nose and the little bright eyes which were crowded close to it, and continued to the upper lip. The nose was very short and pudgy, but the upper lip afforded ample rootage to that immense moustache which was the principal feature of the general's face. At the sides it was drawn up in two prodigious loops that came to sharp points; in front, it descended like a polished ball of darkness and covered a great portion of his lower lip. The lower jaw was a huge foundation, a great and out-jutting rock to support the rest of the structure. But the moustache was always the main feature, and only when the general's laughter or curses blew the black mist of it aside could his mouth be seen clearly; otherwise, speech never quite unsheathed the lower lip.

When he had shrugged his shoulders more snugly into his tight uniform coat the general strode out of the closet which held the safe, and went into the outer rooms.

He was indignant as he saw the crowd which filled the chambers. He felt that the precious hangings had been soiled by the mere proximity of such common fellows as these. And he said to Don Luis, that thin-faced major who had been overseer in the tormenting of Rubriz:

"Clear the rooms!"

It was done at once. Only a few officers remained, and an armed guard outside the broken door. The sign of the shattered wood stirred the general more than bloodshed on a battle-field. It was only when he had seated himself in his big throne-like chair, however, that he began to ask questions.

Sergeant Andres was the first to be called. Black blood was still dried on his wrists. His features remained discoloured. Yet his eyes were clear and courageous.

Because of his courage, rather than his discretion, he told a clear, straightforward story, from the moment when the tapping was heard at the postern to that time when he had nearly suffocated and yet had continued to work at the gag until it was loosened and he was able to cry out for help.

The general said:

"What tapping could have called you out from your post?"

"There is a girl in the *cantina* next to the fort. I told her that if she ever tapped in a certain way, I would speak to her."

The general was so angered that he almost leaped up from his chair. And his officers muttered together, sympathetically.

"That girl," said the general, "is the daughter of Miguel Santos. She is Rosita Santos, eh? Is she behind this deviltry? Has she been sent for?"

"She has been sent for," said Don Luis, nodding.

"Unless she has run for her life, she should be here by this time."

"This sergeant," said the general, in a gentle voice, "at the risk of stifling himself managed at last to give the alarm. Otherwise, who knows what might have happened? For that reason, see that he's paid a hundred pesos. That's a reward for a hero. Also, he was the fool and traitor who let danger into the fort. Because of that, strip the coat from him, tie his hands to his back, and flog him out of the fort and through the town till you've seen the last of him."

A quick smile of appreciation greeted the depth and the wisdom of this judgment. And even Sergeant Andres only rolled up his eyes once to heaven. For he could not even conceive a beating that would not be healed and instantly forgotten for the sake of a hundred silver pesos. So he was swept out of the room.

The general then demanded that the scoundrels who had entered his rooms and locked the door behind them should be produced instantly.

There was no one to produce! The whole of the two rooms had been searched, and nothing had been found. People had even looked out the windows. . . .

"Did you think that they were birds, that you looked out the windows?" shouted the general, so loudly that his moustache was thrown into confusion by his cry. "No, you fools! You rushed into the rooms in a crowd, and the two thieves slipped out from behind curtains and joined you in your search. They milled around with you, like two more head among so many cattle. And then they sneaked away from the fort. They are in some *cantina* now, drinking and laughing at the soldiers of Duraya. The garrison of the fort becomes a laughing-stock. The President will hear of this. All the army will begin to laugh at me—me—me!"

He raised his voice a bit for each of the last three words, until his shout was a hoarse scream. His officers gave back a little. He looked as though he might charge them with his fists at any moment, and he had been known to do such a thing before this.

And then he saw, between two soldiers at the door, the pretty face of Rosita, from the *cantina* of Miguel Santos. Some of his rage disappeared at once. He had her brought in. As he watched her walk forward, he began to forget about everything. Even the emeralds of Our Lady turned into bits of green glass, so far as he was concerned. However, he knew that a good way is to sound the loudest trumpet first.

"To draw soldiers from their duty, that is treason!" he thundered at her. "Do you know the punishment for treason?"

"To be stood against a wall and shot down," said the girl. And she spoke with such a quiet, even voice that Ignacio Estrada was moved.

"You have a story to tell," he said to her. "Every woman can at least tell lies. Come, out with your pack of words."

"I know nothing except poor Sergeant Andres," she said.

"Why do you call him 'poor' Sergeant Andres?"

"They were beating him with whips as I came in through the gate."

"He's your lover, eh?"

"To me he is nothing."

"But you come to tap at the postern when it's his turn to be on guard behind it?" shouted the general.

"I never have tapped at it. He told me how to knock if I wanted him. I never wanted him."

One of the officers bit his lip to the blood to keep from smiling.

"Ah," said the general, "and you sold your information to thieves? Is that it? Thieves and murderers—and you knew them—and you sold the news to them?"

"What did I sell?" said the girl. "The sergeant owed money to a poor man. The poor man could never meet Sergeant Andres to ask for the money that was owing. So I told him how to tap on the postern and how the sergeant would answer him. That is all."

She made a little gesture with both hands, raising her shoulders a trifle. She smiled a bit and shook her head so that all guilt might drop away from her.

"When did you tell this?" asked the general, grimly.

"A week—ten days ago."

"To what man?"

"I never knew his name. But he was drinking in the *cantina* and complaining about Sergeant Andres. That is all."

"Where is he now?"

"How can I tell, Excellency? I only see what comes into the *cantina*, and he has not come there for many days."

"Friends," said the general, suddenly, to his officers, "is she speaking the truth?"

"She is too pretty to tell a lie," answered Don Luis.

The general frowned, and the frown pulled the shag of his black hair down over his eyes.

Then he waved his hand, saying:

"The rest of you leave me. Remain outside the door. I am going to see what the truth of this may be."

He added, with a roar:

"Stop your damned smiling and get out!"

The officers got out in haste, and left Ignacio Estrada alone with the girl.

He pointed to a chair. She thanked him with a little bow and slipped into it. For a time he remained with his thoughts. Then he arose and began to pace up and down the room with his left hand on the hilt of his sword. He knew how to move his hand a little so as to bring from the scabbard an ominous and a martial sound of humming steel. He began to marshal words like soldiers; for he felt that he was about to attack a prize greater to him than any rich city.

CHAPTER XVII

The wind had fallen from a yell to a moan and the rain no longer whipped those aching bodies which remained rigid on the ledge under the windows of the governor's room.

"After a time we'll grow cold and weak enough to fall," said Rubriz to his friend. "And then we'll climb back inside to make a last stand. But we'll be no good, then. It would have been better if we had fought it out in the beginning, when they broke down the door."

He pointed down. Below them went the lights of a patrol. Every few minutes those lights had been passing. The fort of Duraya was as tensely prepared as though a great army were about to rush to the attack, and every man was at his post.

"Still wait for a little," said Montana. His jaws ached with cold as he spoke. The words came shuddering out of his throat. "We still have some part of a long chance."

"What chance?" asked Rubriz.

"One chance brought us up to the governor's rooms. Another chance may get us out of the fort again. Hush! That—that is Rosita!"

There had been a slight lull in the rain again, and he heard the sweet voice of the girl, penetrant because of its high pitch. He worked quickly along the ledge until he was under the window of the bedroom again. He could look in over the sill, while Rubriz was posted on the farther side, whispering:

"Now that he's alone there with the girl—we could leap in and kill him, Montana. That would be worth more than slaughtering a dozen of the soldiers——"

"Hush!" commanded Montana.

The girl had come into the bedroom and was looking quietly around her. Behind her moved the governor, his eyes glittering through the black shagginess of the hair that still pitched from his forehead. General Estrada was excited; but the girl had in her eyes that blank look which the Kid had seen in them once before, as though thought were mastering her senses.

Estrada was saying:

"Now, this isn't a great thing that I'm offering you, Rosita. But there will be other things and other places. Do you think that Duraya is a big enough place to hold me? No; I'll go on to the big cities. They know me —the rest of them know me. I've fought hard enough to get more than this, and I'll fight again when I'm needed. It won't be long. You'll see what will happen, my little friend. Or do you think that my country has forgotten me?"

She turned around and looked up at the general with those blank eyes which were seeing the future, perhaps.

"You are unhappy," said Estrada, "because you have been dragged here by brutes of soldiers, you are unhappy."

"Not because of that," said the girl.

"Love, then?" asked the general, scowling.

She shrugged her shoulders and answered: "Why do you ask all these questions? You are General Estrada. I work in a *cantina*. There is the answer to all the questions at once."

"I don't understand that," the general told her.

"Well," she answered, wearily, "a girl is not pretty for ever. She has to make a bargain. You think a jewel and a carriage—you think that sort of thing is enough. But I'd rather marry a fat merchant and hear him talk about money six days of the week. I'm only young once—and that has to last me for ever."

"Oh-ho!" murmured the general. "Are you talking to me about marriage?"

"I'm talking to you about nothing," said Rosita.

"I could go—a general like Estrada—he could go to some big ranch-owner with a hundred thousand cattle—with rivers and mountains all of his own—a man like Estrada could find a man with a fortune and a daughter. Eh, Rosita?"

"Well, there are plenty of them."

"But let me tell you I am going to be rich in my own right. And then, Rosita—well, I have eyes and I've used them. Do you understand? You are enough for me in yourself."

She jerked around towards him.

"Ah, is it that?" she asked.

"Well, look at me and say something. What do you see?"

"A big moustache," said the girl, calmly.

It seemed to Montana that the general would surely fly into a passion, but he only laughed.

"When I'm on horseback, I look better," he said. "But I'm not beautiful. However, there are beautiful things about me."

"There are the soldiers who are afraid not to follow you," said the girl.

"They have followed me into places, too. They have died like flies around me. Maybe they will die that way again. That is what they are, to me. Flies, now that I am General Estrada. But because they are afraid to run away when I lead them, one day I shall be rich."

"Yes," nodded the girl.

"The finest province in Mexico—I shall ask for it, and it shall be mine. Shall we help ourselves to the plunder, then?"

"We?"

"Yes; you and I. Rosita, I speak from my heart. See what I am; not beautiful; not very young; but strong. There is a brain up here on top of the moustache."

"That is true," she answered.

"A brain clever enough to see that Rosita is worth more than a rich girl. Tell me, then—are we to be married?"

"Well, perhaps we are," she said.

"And then you will stop letting your eyes run this way and that?"

"I'll try to stop," she said. "It's hard to learn all at once."

She was hard as steel, bright as steel, cold as steel. There was no smiling about her, now.

"Then we begin as friends, and hope to end as lovers?" he asked.

"We may end that way," said the girl.

"Time teaches us how to put up with ugly things," said the general. "When you hear the crowd yelling for me and when you see the horse dancing under me, then you will like me much better. But if we are friends, you know that there is no lying between us?"

"No," she agreed. But she frowned.

"Then tell me—was it the truth you spoke to me to-night?"

"No," she said.

A little electric prickling spread across the small of Montana's back.

"I knew it was a lie," said the general, gently. "But truth is always a welcome guest, even when it comes late.

Who was it that you sent to the postern and told about the signal that would bring out the sergeant?"

At this she closed her eyes and bent back her head, as the Kid had seen her do before. But at last she looked at the governor again and said:

"It was a gringo."

"A gringo? And he has come safely into this fort and gone out again?"

"He has stained his skin to make it darker. His hair is black; but his eyes are blue."

"Go on!" urged the general. "I shall have him if I have to ride a thousand miles to get him."

She shook her head.

"Why do you say 'no'?" he demanded. "Listen to me! If it is some outlawed man, I have friends among the bandits, also. I shall use enough money to warm the cold hearts. Before long I shall learn his trail."

"It is El Keed!" she said, almost gloomily.

The anger of Rubriz at this treachery made him actually murmur loud. The Kid gripped his arm to call him back to himself. His own teeth were set. He told himself that he was seeing not Rosita, only, but the hearts of all pretty women.

The general had taken the news like a bullet through the body.

"El Keed?" he repeated, stupidly. "But he is far away in the north. Mexico is closed against him like the teeth of a wolf frozen dead. He will never dare to enter this country again. Some other man has pretended to be El Keed!"

"It is El Keed," she insisted, in that flat voice. "In his own country there is nothing for him to do but sleep and grow fat. That is why he has come into Mexico again."

"But in Duraya—here in my fort—what could he want here?"

"The emerald crown of Our Lady," said the girl.

"Blood of my heart! Blood of Heaven! Blood of my heart!" gasped the general. "Why should he look for that here?"

The girl smiled.

"We are friends—we tell no lies to one another?" said she.

But Estrada had to take a turn or so up and down the room before he could face Rosita once more.

"Come away with me," he told her. "I shall send you safely home. There are many things for me to do. If the gringo devil and robber has been inside the fort —if he has smelled the way—Rosita, you have told me more than the value of life. Come quickly!"

They went off together, and the muttering voice of the general rolled indistinctly over his shoulder:

"El Keed—in Duraya! Blood of my heart, what man would believe it?"

Rubriz and Montana stood again in the bedroom of the general, and the bandit wasted one moment to say to his friend:

"There is your lesson! If you must have women, give them your hand—but only with gold in it. Give trust to them and you give it to the wind!"

"We have work to do," said the Kid through his teeth.

And he went straight for the closet in which they had found the safe of Ignacio Estrada. The teeth of Montana were still set hard and something that was not quite a smile kept lifting his lip a trifle.

When they were inside the closet, Rubriz could hear his friend humming that old, old song:

Love is not happiness.
A horse under heel ;
A sword under hand ;
And red wine for the belly ;
But love is not happiness.

Rubriz himself joined in the humming, very softly. The two of them fell to work with the skill of old practitioners.

CHAPTER XVIII

Suppose a sound as of two immense hands clapped together, in such a fashion that the air is not struck out flatlings, in a thunderclap. Suppose a pair of huge doors hurled down on a thick carpet. Imagine a quivering shock that runs through a building and seems to come from any direction at all—the sides, the bottom, the top. That was what the explosion was like in Fort Duraya. Nearly every soul in the big building heard it or felt it, for it was almost more to be felt than to be heard. A good many thought that it was a severe earthquake. Most men looked at one another, startled, and muttered, "There's something wrong!" There were very few who could guess that it was actually an explosion.

The general, Ignacio Estrada, was one of these. He had brought Rosita to the gate of the fort, on his arm, so that she had nothing to do except to saunter down the short slope towards the lights of the town. In front of the entire guard at the gate, he leaned and kissed the girl. She received that caress on a brow of stone, and the general would not have been surprised if he had heard a snicker from one of the men.

"Well, Rosita," he said to her, "one of these days you will like me better."

"I shall pray," she answered. She looked right back at him. He did not know whether to curse her insolence or damn her stupidity. Then he decided that he would do neither, but begin to use all of his brains in the study of her. For one thing, she had taken on a highly additional significance, simply because he knew that she had seen El Keed face to face, perhaps had smiled and laughed with that fantastic adventurer. She startled the good general as though he had discovered, in some plain, drab woman of middle age, the widow of a great man. For El Keed was great in the eyes of General Estrada In part the greatness was based upon a mystery. Estrada could understand why men should dare greatly for great rewards, but to ride into danger merely for the sake of danger's face was an absurdity and a madness.

These were the thoughts that were working in the mind of the governor as he said good-bye to the girl, and at that moment he heard from somewhere inside the fort—or was it not from the ground beneath him?— that soft, thick, muffled explosion. He started. He looked wildly at Rosita.

"What is it?" she asked him.

"El Keed—I think, El Keed!" said the governor.

"Inside the fort?" she gasped. "*Still* inside the fort?"

She even made a pace or two in pursuit of the general, but Estrada was making off at full speed, shouting to the officer of the gate:

"Sound the alarm! Every man at his post! Sound the alarm!"

That was why Montana and Rubriz did not have much time.

They had watched the fire run down the fuse under the door of the closet. They had heard the very light crackling and spitting sound which the fuse made. They lay flat on the floor in a corner of the bedroom and waited. All sound ended.

"The cursed fuse was wet—it was ruined!" growled Rubriz. "That dog of an Oñate shall learn what it is to give me false material!"

Then the explosion came. It blew the door of the closet shuddering open. An invisible puff, as it were, of thick, strange-smelling air rolled out to them, and the flame jumped wildly in the lamp and almost went out.

When they got into the closet they found the door of the safe open and hanging by only one hinge!

Well, let them take this much good fortune almost for granted—since they were not yet clear of the fort! Even if the emerald crown were in their hands, they had not gained it until they were out of Fort Duraya.

That was why they said nothing when from the second or third drawer they opened they took a soft wrapping of chamois. It fell open in their hands and they saw the green glinting of the emeralds, like the eyes of cats when a torch reflects from them by night.

Then they heard the shrill neighing of the alarm bugle that was blowing from the gate of the fort and causing the echoing of trampling feet to sound in immediate answer from the barracks and all through the big building.

"Now—*amigo*—for the last step!" said Rubriz.

He took one-half of the broken crown and gave the other to his friend.

"Ay," said Montana. "One of us may stick in the trap. Take some of this stuff."

He had picked two soft, heavy little bags of gold out of another drawer of the safe. Rubriz dropped one into a pocket of his trousers. Montana put the little ten-pound weight inside his coat.

"The best way is right back to the postern by which we came in. Follow me there, Rubriz."

"Back the same way? They will have it crowded with armed men."

"I tell you that's the safest chance."

"Montana, it is no chance at all!"

They were in the bedroom of the governor again. They were in the closet opposite to that which had held the safe, and while Rubriz completed his costume by huddling swiftly into a white shirt which he snatched from a shelf, Montana picked a great cloak from its hanger and flung it around his shoulders.

They sprang out again into the open room.

"Rubriz, I tell you I have a lucky feeling. Come with me to-night!"

"In the name of God, Montana—quickly!—to me, *amigo* !"

A voice called out distantly. Then a door opened and there was a sudden rushing of footfalls, close at hand, at the very entrance to the bedchamber.

Montana, springing for the door that led into the little side corridor, could not believe himself when he saw Rubriz rush straight forward to encounter this overwhelming danger.

Well, mere physical resistance could not be in the head of the Mexican. He must have thought out some cunning device.

So Montana went rapidly through the corridor. He came out cautiously into the officers' mess-hall. Two or three chairs were overturned. He found himself, against his own belief, pausing to finish off a brimming glass of wine.

But, after all, the matter of a few seconds here and there would be of no importance. He might as well pause for a cigarette. It would even help him.

Considering this, he actually lighted a smoke and then went on again.

The bugles were still going, the sound penetrating the thick walls dimly, entering the mind like persistent needles of thought. But not even the thickness of the walls could keep out the damned rattling and clamouring and crazy rhythms of the alarm bells. The building seemed to tremble as the sounds found physical root in the foundations of the old fort. And a crazy panic ran out through the blood of Montana and into his brain.

He took hold of that panic with his hands, so to speak, and cast it out of his breast.

His hat was well over his head, well down on the forehead. The flap of the cloak would cover most of the rest of his face. And bluff would have to do the rest—bluff no wider than the edge of a knife. A tight wire to walk across a gulf.

He felt like that. But there was no use weighing things. When there is nothing left but an absurdity, an absurdity is better than nothing.

He reached the stairs that slanted steeply down through the walls. Someone came running up towards him, almost crashed into him at the first level landing. The soldier jumped back against the wall.

"Pardon, señor!" he gasped.

Montana went silently past. His hands were under his cloak and the ashes from his cigarette dribbled down.

He was down the second flight of stairs. He was at the entrance to the guardroom.

There had been three men in the place when he and Rubriz made their entrance, terrible hours before. There were almost a dozen present now, and there was a captain among them!

From the deeps of his throat the Kid summoned a

guttural roar: "Attention!" and strode in on the wings of that word.

They came to rigid attention, all of them, their eyes foolishly staring, their arms foolishly stiff at their sides. So the Kid crossed to the door.

"Open!" he thundered.

"But, Excellency——" said the captain.

There was a corporal who heard the word "excellency" and sprang like a frightened rabbit to do the first bidding. He worked feverishly, wrenching back the three bolts. He thrust them so fast and hard that they clanged loudly. The heavy door yawned a little.

"Excellency——" said the captain.

"Silence!" roared El Keed.

"Silence be damned!" exclaimed the captain. "What are you and who are you?"

He came striding, with a jingle of spurs, and the Kid leaped through the widening lip of the door.

The night struck at him like a wet black hand. He heard, from behind him, a scream of rage and astonishment like the shriek of a woman.

Hard to the left he turned, shedding the encumbering cloak as he ran. Behind him, the arm of light was widening, reaching into the rain of the night. And the guard was pouring out, each man shooting at the brilliant phantom nothingness of the light and the rain.

Then they had sight of Montana to their left, already dim with night and distance, and running straight down the slope towards those willows which stood by the bank of the river. They paused even now to fire a few shots, in hope of good fortune and also to catch the ear of the rest of the fort. Then they burst into pursuit of a fugitive who was already invisible.

One cry came out of the throat of the Kid as he neared the willows. And when he came through them he found the gigantic form of the friar. The Kid leaped on the red mare.

"Take the black and the mule," he commanded. "I have half of the crown. The soldiers are after me. We must ford the river. Rubriz will never come this way to-night!"

They pushed straight out from the trees into the water. The rain, sent out of a kind heaven, the same wind and rain that had tortured Montana on the ledge beneath the window, now stormed down in an impenetrable veil. He could hear gunshots from behind, but he could see nothing. The water rose to his knees. It shoaled. He came out on the farther shore, with Brother Pascual beside him.

CHAPTER XIX

As Montana had guessed, it was not on the strength of his hands that Rubriz was depending when he determined to leave the governor's room by the open way.

When he came to the fallen door, he picked it up and placed the burden of it over his shoulder and the back of his neck. He had barely put the thing in position when many men stormed in from the hall with panting General Ignacio Estrada at their head.

He caught Rubriz by the shoulder. His grip slipped on the great, rubbery muscles that shod the bones of Rubriz.

"What's this? What's happening here?" cried Estrada.

"I carry away the door to be repaired," said Rubriz. "I know nothing but orders. I am a poor mozo, señor."

"All half-wits; all fools. Nothing but blind men around me to-night," shouted Estrada.

He strode on into his room. The others followed, and with the bugles blowing the call to arms, Rubriz went on down the stairs.

The governor, entering his bedroom, looked wildly around him. But nothing was wrong. The door of the closet that contained the precious safe was closed. All was apparently well.

"Your eyes! Your eyes!" he shouted to the men around him. "If you have eyes, tell me what they see!"

"There is rather an odd odour in the air," said one of the officers.

"The damned mouldy smell always blows up with a storm out of this old rat-trap!" declared the general.

"There is this black burn on the carpet," said another officer.

"Burn on the carpet? What burn, you fool?" bellowed the general.

Then he saw it, and followed the irregular course of the little black spots to the point where they disappeared under the door of the closet. At that, a suspicion too terrible to pass up into words overwhelmed him. He passed a hand across his shaggy hair.

It seemed to him that a ghost, not Ignacio Estrada, had been rejoicing himself not long before with the pretty face of a girl. Compared with such a loss as might befall him, what were all the women of the world?

He tore open the closet door. Inside, the thick, strange smell which had been noticeable in the bedroom was much more pronounced. And the door of the safe hung open on one hinge—the drawers had been jerked out, half the contents scattered, half taken!

He had a good hold on the edge of the door or he would have staggered. He might even have fallen to his knees under the weight of this calamity. Instead, he merely rolled back his head and stared upwards.

"Father in heaven, what have I done to you?" muttered Estrada.

He turned slowly on the others.

"Get out into every corner of the building!" he exclaimed. "Burrow into the cracks of the stones. Because El Keed is here among us. My God! how can a man walk invisible? I am robbed. Do you hear? And El Keed——"

A loud and sustained rattling of guns began at this moment. The general ran to the open window and leaned out.

"It's from the postern! If the thief has escaped by the way he came, I'll skin them and eat them with my own teeth!"

"No, Excellency. He could not have gone that way. I myself posted ten men and Captain——"

"Damn the men—damn the captains! Names are no good. Numbers are nothing. Brains are what rule the world. Scatter! Use your feet if you can't use your wits!"

The door was heavy, but Rubriz could have carried it like a feather if he had not known that it was better to assume the swinging, slow pace of a true labourer. So he went patiently down the stairs, and through the lower gallery, and finally into the great open courtyard, where he was shocked by a noise of firing just outside the fort and a clamouring of voices made high and thin by excitement.

He dropped the door to the ground, but noticing that some soldiers were watching him, he hastily put it on his back once more and went on.

Had they captured Montana?

Well, at least the curse of the alarm bell was still in his ear, beating on his brain with the impulse to flee as fast as he could. He kept to his steady gait right across the inside parade-ground. He was right at the gate before he was halted.

"Who goes there?"

"Luis Lapaz."

"What's that?"

"The door of the room of General Estrada."

"What are you doing with the door of the commander?" asked the lieutenant. He began to laugh as he asked the question.

"I am carrying it," said Rubriz, simply.

"I can see you are, donkey. But why are you carrying it?"

"I am taking it away," said Rubriz.

"Be patient, *amigo*," said another young officer. "You can see that the man is not right, up here."

"Well, these fools! Luis Lapaz?"

"Yes, señor."

"Where is your pass?"

"I lost it, my señor."

"Come, come! Simpleton or no simpleton, that won't do here! Where did you lose it?"

"And where did you come by a silk shirt, by God!" asked another.

Rubriz looked askance at the great gate. But it was closed, and before he could scale it they would have their bullets in him.

"I lost the pass and my own shirt dancing for the officers," said Rubriz.

"Hai! Are you the one?"

They both began laughing. But the common soldiers, their faces like wood, showed no wish to smile.

Rubriz set his teeth over a groan of rage.

"They tore my own shirt to pieces and beat me, and made me dance on a table," he said. "They kept time with their whips. Then one of them gave me this shirt. He said it would make me a great man in the town. But about that I cannot tell."

"Why can't you tell? Was there ever a shirt like that in your family before?"

"That is why my wife will ask me many questions, señor."

They began to laugh again. The clamouring of the alarm bell made the laughter seem a screaming madness.

"Well, open the gate for him before the weight of the door breaks his back for him."

"The sergeant has the key. Sergeant, open the gate for Luis Lapaz!"

The sergeant came out of the little sentry-box beside the gate. He was a big, slow-moving, rigid man. He looked like a foreign soldier, not like one of the homely Mexican troops. He set the key into the lock and then gave his shoulder to the gate. It wavered at the top before it began to sag open, slowly. Rubriz, turning his head away from the sergeant, holding his breath, thought that the gate would never open wide enough for him to pass through.

Suddenly the sergeant exclaimed:

"Turn your head! Look at me! You, I mean—porter, turn your head to me!"

Well, the scar had been covered with deep stain. It would not show, and the little rubber pads that swelled out the lips might be alteration enough to deceive even a man like this sergeant. Or would he remember that night in the mountains when he had been impressed to act as guide through the middle of a storm, when the men of Rubriz were fleeing from Rurales?

So, slowly, Rubriz turned his head, keeping it bowed down low under the door that weighted his shoulders.

The sergeant jumped straight up into the air. With one hand he caught at his stomach. With the other he snatched out the revolver which was holstered well down on his thigh.

"Rubriz!" he shouted. "Rubriz! Rubriz!"

Rubriz flung the door at the sergeant and toppled both him and one of the officers. Then he leaped through the widening gap of the gate—and straight into a column of three squads who were coming up to the entrance of the fort!

He plunged through them like a bull through rushes. Certainly he would have broken away even then, except that the very smallest man of that little column, as he fell, grappled blindly and caught with both arms one of Rubriz' legs.

The bandit went down.

When he rose again, twenty men were spilling over him. Once and again he scattered them as a swimmer might scatter water, but the little bulldog who lay on the ground anchored that one leg which he could grab.

Then the arms of Rubriz were mastered. That was how the miracle happened beyond the belief of any man—that Mateo Rubriz was taken prisoner standing, without a wound on his body, without dealing the slightest damage to any man except for a few bruises.

They tied his hands behind his back. They tied each arm to a guard. They hobbled his feet. In this fashion they led him back through the gate.

The news had gone down the brief slope to the town. The noise of it could be heard passing like a wave all through Duraya.

Mateo Rubriz was captured!

This day which had dawned so bright and which had closed in the double darkness of night and rain, this was the famous day, after all, of the capture of Mateo Rubriz at last. It had seemed that his story would run on for ever, but this was the ending of it.

Up the slope from the town hundreds of people came. They were wild-eyed, and they looked rather frightened than jubilant. The soldiers closed the gate of the fort suddenly in their faces. For one could not tell what would happen when the common people saw their hero in trouble. He might be a double-devil to the prosperous miners and the cattle-owners and the great government officials in their progresses through the land, but he was doer of good to the poor. He was true *"bandido"!*

In the meantime, officers were running. Squads of soldiers were coming up. There in the rain on the parade-ground they searched him and found the little sack of gold, ten pounds of it. Also, they found a small arc of goldwork set with five big emeralds, like the eyes of a cat!

CHAPTER XX

THAT same Major Luis Alvarez who had flogged Rubriz and made him dance was the officer of highest rank among those who conducted the search of Mateo Rubriz in the rain. And the clever brain which was hidden in his narrow forehead above his narrow face was struck through with an inspiration the instant that he saw the five big emeralds and the arc of heavy gold.

The obvious thing was to carry the treasure at once back to the good Bishop Emiliano. The less obvious thing was to report the finding and deliver the jewels to General Ignacio Estrada. People had been whispering some odd things about him, and the famous robbery of the Church of Our Lady. And no sooner had Major Alvarez seen the treasure than he straightway pocketed it and exclaimed, loudly:

"This is stuff worthy of going before the general. Have we found the church-robber, at last? Forward march!"

That was how he marched Rubriz away in search of the general.

The general himself was not in the fort, for the moment. He was out on one of his big chargers, leading a search in person through the wet willows beside the river, though every inch of the ground had already been trampled over long before this by the eager soldiers.

The fury of the general was so great that it left him calm. He wanted to order the instant execution of all the officers in the guardroom by the postern gate. And then he would order that the postern itself should be walled up solidly.

His fury was strangely qualified, none the less. For he could not help remembering that it was through this same postern that he had led ten masked men, on a certain night, into the town and towards the Church of Our Lady of Guadalupe.

When Major Alvarez met him and saluted, with information, the general merely snarled:

"El Keed—tell me that you have him in chains or tell me nothing!"

"No," said the major, with the calm of one who cannot lose as the game is being played; "I can only report that I have Mateo Rubriz!"

Even the thought of the Kid, and even the memory of the jewels, were dimmed for a moment in the mind of the general. It was true that he loved money, but he loved reputation, equally. In a sense, he felt that money could be turned into reputation, and reputation into money. The words were synonyms to him. He got hold of the major and shook him by the shoulders as a school master might shake a child.

"Say the thing slowly. Look me in the eye. If you are drunk again and speaking like this, I'll have you shot, Major!"

Alvarez had been drawn quite close by the grip of the general, and now he murmured:

"Out of the pocket of Rubriz, some goldwork and five big emeralds——"

"Five?" muttered the general. "Only five? But that's half. Mateo Rubriz and five—five of the lost—— Why, it's better this way! Tell me, Alvarez! Did other eyes see those emeralds?"

"The moment I saw them my hand was over them.

Not three men could have seen, and those three won't believe to-morrow what they saw to-night."

"Alvarez, I've noted you down for a long time. A man of brains. A man of action with your hands and not with your tongue!"

At that the face of Alvarez actually puckered with delight. Its thinness turned into breadth, like the face of a cat.

The thing was arranged quietly. General Estrada sat in his own study and Alvarez stood before him. Upon the table Alvarez laid down the little pouch of heavy gold. He laid, also, the arc of metalwork which had five points, with an emerald in each one—a big, shining emerald.

"You are going to be rewarded, Alvarez," said the general. "If you should become a colonel, suddenly, would it surprise you?"

"Have I not heard a rumour about your kindness, sir?" answered Alvarez. "But also I was noticing that there are *five* emeralds."

"Five?" said the general. "There are ten—but only five in this damned broken fragment——"

He felt that he was talking on a little too freely. No matter what Alvarez might guess, there was no use confirming him in such plain words. So he broke off, scowling a little.

"What I noticed," said Alvarez, "is that five makes an odd number, whereas ten—or four—is exactly even."

The hint was very broad, but the general could not see or understand, without too much pain. Therefore, he only looked wistfully at Major Alvarez, as though at a figure far away. The wind had changed, clearing the sky and letting the moon shine through. The general now turned his head and looked, with a sigh, at the moon-brightened heavens. The strength of his sigh parted the dense brush of his moustache and allowed his pouting lips to be seen, and the full majesty of that enormous chin.

"Five!" muttered the general.

"Whereas four," said the major, gently persistent, "would make an exactly even number."

With his strong fingers, slowly, the general broke away an emerald from its setting at the end of the arc. He dropped the jewel into the palm of his hand. As part of the crown it had been beautiful, but seen by itself its beauty increased strangely. Its green fire filled the mind of Estrada like the majesty of the ocean, with all its fleets of treasure journeying across that broad bosom.

He closed his eyes and held out his hand.

Delicately as a bird could pick up a grain, the cold finger-tips of the major removed the emerald from the hot hand of Estrada.

Well, there would be a chance, one day, to silence this man's tongue—for ever.

"As a matter of fact," said the major, looking down at the emerald, "it is easy to see that this is only a paste imitation."

"Ha?" cried Estrada.

"I mean," said Alvarez, "a man with the proper sort of an eye can see that it is not the jewel that was stolen from the church in Duraya."

Estrada leaned back in his chair with a sigh.

"I understand you," he said.

"Therefore, when I drop a word here and there that what Rubriz had was no part of the stolen treasure, that the poor fool for once had lost his eye and merely picked up glass——"

"Very well," said the general, wearily.

And his glance followed the movement with which Alvarez carelessly dropped the gem into a pocket.

"Any other orders, sir?" asked Alvarez.

"Yes, go down to the old dungeon. Pick out the wettest cell and—prepare the place. I may have to be doing a little questioning before long. Also, have that girl—that Rosita—brought to me at once."

Alvarez saluted decorously and withdrew at once. He did not need to be told that full noon was striking on the brightest day of his life. It was an opportunity which would have to be handled carefully, but he was certain that he would be able to rise to every occasion. Great men cannot help hating those who are useful to them; nevertheless, they also cannot help advancing them. Alvarez felt that the promotion was already his. He walked away through Fort Duraya with the bearing of one who is above correction and close to the command.

CHAPTER XXI

If the brain of Estrada was not the most astute in the world, it was nevertheless extremely strong because it was extremely simple. When he saw his ends, he went straight to them; and the advantage which he saw now before him was that, in possessing the person of Rubriz he also possessed a very distinct claim upon the remaining five emeralds.

El Keed must have the missing fragment. El Keed it was who had walked through that chosen guard at the postern and made fools of the soldiery. The entire manœuvre was covered with his trade-mark of brazen effrontery. But Rubriz must have some meeting-place appointed with his comrade. Somewhere they were to join together. Instead of Rubriz at that meeting-place, the men of General Estrada would appear!

Rosita was brought in a hurry. Mateo Rubriz was marched into the room between two guards. He was not as tall as either of them, but he made them insignificant: as a little, frail, skinny pair of natives would look beside a huge gorilla from the African forest. His manner was calmly composed. His eye was full, open, direct. When he spoke there was no tremor of his voice. No one could have guessed that his last chances of living were passing away.

Estrada said, "Rosita, this is not the man you thought to be El Keed?"

"No," said the girl.

"Do you know who this is? Have you never seen him before?"

"Never before. But I think I've seen pictures of a man who has been kind to the poor—Mateo Rubriz!"

She drew a little towards him as she spoke. Rubriz spat at her.

"Strike him on the mouth!" commanded Estrada.

"No, in the name of Heaven!" said the girl.

The soldier, his fist raised, looked with an inquiring grin at his commander, and Estrada in turn stared at the girl. He found her very much altered. She was paler. And the smile that had been on her lips for years was entirely gone. She looked like an older sister of that Rosita he had known. She looked like a woman who has borne children and lost them.

"Let Rubriz be," said Estrada. "You can go, Rosita. You are only sure that you never saw this man before? He was not the one to whom Sergeant Andres owed money? If you saw El Keed, you did not see him with this Rubriz?"

"No," said the girl.

She was turning away when Rubriz said to her:

"Take a gift from me away with you, sweetheart. A curse on your pretty little face. May the smallpox bite white holes in it!"

"Beat that mouth of his shut!" yelled Estrada, in one of his furies.

The guard struck Rubriz full on the mouth, but the bleeding lips spoke on:

"No man for your heart, traitor; no child for your womb; no priest for your grave!"

The fist struck again, but Mateo Rubriz laughed, and his laughter blew out a fine spray of his blood. Rosita had slunk out of the room, her hands pressed over her ears.

"Is Rubriz chained?" asked Estrada.

"See, Excellence."

Estrada, with a sense of luxurious content, surveyed the heavy chains that weighed down the hands of Rubriz. There was an iron ball of twenty pounds' weight hitched to his ankles, and the chain from the ball passed up by a special chain and was fastened to a collar that fitted close around that great neck.

"Leave him, then," said Estrada. "I may need you again in a moment. Wait outside the room."

When they had withdrawn, Estrada said:

"Rubriz, the fact is that you worked with El Keed. You made a gringo your partner to steal from me to-day."

Rubriz said nothing. There was merely a sort of idle curiosity in the eyes with which he scanned the face of the general. But in Estrada there was a mighty confidence. It was as large as his soul and rooted as deep.

"When you stole the emeralds," said Estrada, "you took half and El Keed took half. You went by different ways. And, by God! you almost escaped, as he did. Bad luck stopped you. And yet, Rubriz, it may not be such very bad luck, after all. You have fallen into the hands of a man of understanding. I know your life. I know what you have done. Your fingers have been on the throttles of some of the rich. But the poor have never had any reason to fear you. Now then, I was once a poor man, myself. I remember those days very well; and I want to tell you that I can feel a sympathy for you. Such a sympathy that I could give up all the noise and the reputation that will come to me from all over Mexico because I am the man whose grip at last closed on you. I could arrange matters so that you would be able to slip quietly away, Rubriz, one of these nights. And all that I want you to leave behind for me is a little information—just a little information, Rubriz."

He went over to his cabinet, selected a bottle with care, brought it with a glass to his desk. He filled the glass, lighted a cigar, and began to turn the smoke in his mouth and sip the brandy. The warmth of the liquor was no greater than the surety which possessed the soul of the general.

"Something for nothing is not what a man can expect in this world, Rubriz. But the payment I ask from you is very small: I begin by pointing out to you that there are certain jewels in the hands of El Keed—that El Keed was your partner in the work of this night. I merely ask you where I can find the gringo."

There was no answer.

The general said:

"You note, Rubriz, that the man is not one of us. You note that he is a gringo?"

Rubriz smiled. And at that, with a touch of anger in his voice for the first time, the general continued:

"If you will talk willingly you receive your freedom. But if you put me to it—if I have to tear the answers out of you, I shall have them, with blood dripping from every word of them. You hear me, Rubriz?"

General Ignacio Estrada could not believe his eyes. Yet he saw that the prisoner continued to regard him in silence, without greater emotion than a mild curiosity. The general leaped to his feet.

"You fool!" he shouted. "Do you know what I am?"

"A dog and the son of a dog," said Rubriz.

Not for the first time that night, the rage of the general was so great that he remained calm. He swallowed the rest of his cognac and let the taste of it mingle with his cold fury. Then he called in the guards.

In a sense it would be better this way. More than once General Estrada had enjoyed putting his questions by force, but he had never had such a complete man to deal with. There was pleasure as well as answers to be extracted by the method he had in view. Therefore he almost wondered that he had, in the first place, offered any sort of a bargain to Rubriz.

The little cell in that old dungeon which was supposed to be disused was the lowest of the entire cellar of the building. It was so low that the river water, seeping aslant through the soil, kept oozing through the walls and covering them with mould. And on the floor there was slime from which sprang up a disgusting odour of decay. But though the irons were thick with scales of rust, they retained a strong core.

By pulleys, and by ropes which were fastened to the iron rings at the base of the opposite walls and also to the feet and the hands of Mateo Rubriz, his body had been stretched taut. After that, in order to increase the strain, a low hurdle had been passed beneath his huge, naked body. He was now left alone with the general, who had for his equipment only some buckets of perfectly innocent water and a large leather funnel.

The general did not begin at once. He first admired the immense strength of the body of his victim, the great thews and sinews pulled so tight that they stood out in a high relief. It reminded the general of the strings of a musical instrument, properly tuned. So was Rubriz tuned, and Estrada felt that he knew how to extract the most exquisite pain.

"After so many days in the desert, after so many hot days with sand in the face and the throat, what could be better for you than a little water, Rubriz?" asked the general. "And you shall have some. You shall have such a drink as you never tasted before. We begin with a drink, and afterwards we ask a few questions. But when you are willing to talk, you can signify by the lifting of one finger. For I shall be watching, my friend!"

With that, he pried open the jaws of Rubriz, using a cold chisel as a leverage for that purpose. Then into the gullet of the prisoner he forced the small end of the big leather funnel. Out of the nearest bucket he fiiled the funnel, and stepped back to wait.

Gradually the liquid ran down into the body of Rubriz. Stretched to rigidity as it was, the least pressure from within was a frightful agony.

It was that old torture called "the question"; of all abominations the most terrible gift from brute to brute in the history of man. With that device, more frightful than all instruments for tearing flesh or bruising bones, murderers in the old days were given the pains of ten deaths before the law permitted them to expire under the merciful hand of the executioner. All the great nerves of lungs and intestines and heart, every inward fibre of the body, was slowly ground and tormented, one by one and altogether. The greatest "question" for female malefactors was limited to six quarts. For men, it was the pleasure of the torturer which set the limit.

And the governor, looking down at the immense bulk of his victim, felt that the limit could be very great indeed.

He filled the funnel again, and watched the liquid work like twisting fists inside the body of Rubriz. He stood directly above the face of the man, so that Rubriz could not help but look back into his eyes. He saw the sweat brighten the face of the outlaw, and the perfect agony brighten his eyes.

A thin tremor of joy, like sound, ran through the body and the heart of Estrada. He leaned still closer and forced his gaze into the eyes of Rubriz.

He could gain no real satisfaction in this manner, however. For the agony of Rubriz did not seem increased by this personal supervision of his pains.

Estrada sent down another funnelful of water. He could see the whole body of his victim begin to work now. And presently, almost beyond his hope, he could hear the voice of groaning agony. He thought for a moment that it was the appeal for mercy. When he saw that it was merely the involuntary reaction that accompanied breathing, the face of the general grew black with an almost virtuous anger.

Rubriz had begun to wish for death. He wished for it more passionately than he ever had wished for another thing in his life. There was no part of his body that was not in pain. The frightful drawing of the ropes cut into his wrists, into his feet and ankles. Bones might be broken under the strain, but the numbness and the agony combined so that he could not even particularize the regions of the torment. Sometimes it was ice that filled his veins, and then it was swelling fire. And then it was the pure essence of pain, and nothing else except that frightful and increasing nausea.

General Estrada was no longer calmly contented. He had begun to curse. More than once he beat the body of his victim with his fists. And every stroke left a great, swelling, purple mark on the tensed flesh.

And then, lifting the eyelids of Rubriz, he saw that the life was ebbing rapidly out of the body. And without speech—without one word of entreaty—without a single lament other than that groaning, stertorous breathing over which Rubriz had no control.

One more dose of water to flow into the distorted body and there would be an end, but the general did not wish it to be so. He had staked his cards on his immense surety, and his threats and his tortures had drawn only one speech from the outlaw. He had called Estrada a dog and a son of a dog. And now he was to die—triumphant.

It was against this triumph in death that the soul of the general revolted.

And then he told himself, in an interval of impassioned cursing, that he had been a fool to think that he could wear down such a spirit as that of Rubriz in a single session.

No, little by little the steel of this spirit must be ground away until it was thin and brittle enough to snap under a finger's weight. And when the general considered how the grinding should be performed, he could think of only one safe and perfect place, because there was only one ultimate, man-made hell on earth.

That was the Valley of the Dead, from which fools whispered that Miguel Santos had escaped.

They were fools because no man ever escaped from the Valley. And that was the perfection of its hell—its hopelessness. Out of its bounds no one was ever pardoned, because the tales which could have been told by the saved would have blackened the face of the entire world.

And when the general arrived at this conclusion, he looked suddenly up with an exaltation of his spirit.

There is no absolute hate without fear intermingled, and during the long process of the torture, he had begun to hate his victim because he could not help being struck through with a cold apprehension now and again: suppose that the man should live—should contrive an escape from the fort—should be able at some time to come inside its boundaries once more——

Well, the Valley of the Dead could receive him and hold him for ever.

Should not such be the fate of those weaker creatures who venture to oppose men of destiny, like Ignacio Estrada?

CHAPTER XXII

FOR one whole day Montana fled into the mountains away from Duraya. Then, for two days, he lived a quiet, idyllic life in the wilderness. He had found a bit of a valley, above timber line, where the forage was good for Sally and where he himself could catch fat fish out of a foolishly small creek.

He would lie prone for hours under the shade of a rock during the day. He had that rare faculty of stopping all thought, almost all sensation, and permitting the river of time to pick up the soul and carry it slow or fast through strange countries.

At night he built two small fires of brush and lay between them, warm, comfortable on a bed of leaves and wiry little bushes. And since he did most of his sleeping during the day, he spent the night gazing at the stars and letting whatever thoughts might come roll painlessly into his mind—and out again. Or else he would go with Sally for a careless cruise through the plateaux of that high country where the keen sweetness of the air gave to the body a sense of spiritual purity. The rider was always at ease on those journeys because the wild mare was capable of being the guide and the scout. To her ears all the mountain sounds had a special meaning. To her nostrils the mountain scents conveyed subtle volumes. She knew at what hour the wolf had passed and where the mountain lion had crouched and where the evil little coyotes had trotted. So she went warily on her way, picking her steps, loving the air of danger around her. Then they would return to the embers of the fires, and the master would let the world drift past him again.

But at the end of the third day since the flight from Duraya, he turned back again towards the town.

A steady preoccupation made a dark undercurrent continually in his mind.

Where was Rubriz? What had happened to him? The question would lift him from sleep to wakefulness in the middle of the night, and it rode behind him all day long.

That sense of duty unperformed was not a familiar thing to Montana. He had lived as free as the wind; but savage Mateo Rubriz had laid a grip on his mind and his heart. He had to return the treasure that was in his possession; but above all, he had to find out what had become of his companion in the robbery.

He took two days, coming down from his high place. And once a day, at high noon, he took the golden ornament with the emeralds in the palm of his hand. He turned it so that the jewels flickered and glared at him like a five-eyed cat, and then he put the thing away again in its chamois wrapping.

He wondered how long it would take for the jewels to enter his blood and become a necessity to him? As to his strength to resist, he knew that there was a border and a boundary beyond which he could not pass. That was why he was glad to see Duraya, white as snow, with the sunset gold of its river looped around.

He left the mare in a hollow at the verge of the town and made her lie down. There she would remain, according to his teaching, like a young faun left by its mother, until he came again.

And he went on into the town in the early night, forgetting all dangers, gladdening himself with the sounds of human beings again, and the scent of the pungent Mexican cookery.

It was a night of festival. The entire population had gathered in the street that ran past the fort, past the church, past the bishop's palace. So he made a half-mask from the lining of his coat and entered the current of noise which flowed along the street. At last he came to the bishop's palace and from the doorway looked back on the scene, the lanterns, the laughter, the faces whose joy could not be masked.

He forgot his danger still farther. It was a cold stream, but it was no higher than his ankles. He began to laugh, himself, and he was still laughing as he went up the stairs.

He knew the way—Brother Pascual had told him about it—so he turned right in at the open door of the bishop's room and found that good little man at the window—not at devotion, but leaning his elbows on the high sill and shaking his head at the bright procession which moved beneath him.

When he heard the laughter of that young voice behind him, he turned a trifle and said, "Why do you laugh, my son?"

"Because when I came across the street," said Montana, "I heard an old man and a young boy singing the same song, and his voice was squeaking so high that it sounded as small as the boy's."

"What song were they singing?"

"They were singing this:

> "*The devil came to the earth one day*
> *And saw Alicia over the way*——"

"Hush!" said the bishop. "Why are you here?"

"I've come to ask you where I can find a friend of mine, and to give you a little token you've been missing."

"A token?" asked the bishop.

As the youth came closer to him, Bishop Emiliano lifted his gleaming bald head higher and higher until he was staring up into the masked face.

"I beg your pardon," said the Kid. "Of course I know that there's no harm can come from you." He took off his mask.

"But who are you, my son?" said the bishop.

"Perhaps you'll find my name engraved somewhere on this?" said Montana.

And he put the trinket in the chamois wrapping into the hands of the bishop. The latter, unwrapping the thing slowly, still kept his grave, gentle eyes fixed on the stranger until something that his fingers touched made him look down quickly.

Then he saw that sacred glimmer of gold and green and he clasped the treasure in both hands against his breast.

"*You* are El Keed!" he said. "Ah, where is Pascual? He knew that you would come back and bring this. He was sure of it. He gave me his oath that there was no evil in you, my son."

"Oh, there's trouble enough in me!" said the Kid.

"What shall I do for you?" asked the bishop, making a helpless gesture. "How shall I make you a reward? You are not of our faith, my son?"

"No," said the Kid; "never mind about the rewards. Give them to Rubriz; give them to Mateo. A few Aves will make him feel richer than a king."

Then he saw something in the face of the priest and went a bit closer to him.

"There's one thing that I could use," he said. "It's never happened to me before, and perhaps it might as well happen now. Give me your blessing, if you will."

He kneeled down suddenly. The good bishop was

taken aback for an instant, and he peered down at the Kid as though he suspected, for a moment, that there might be a bit of sacrilegious mockery in this gesture, but the strong, clean features of the Kid were no longer smiling.

At that, Bishop Emiliano put both hands on the head of Montana.

"Our Father in heaven," he said, "give faith and love to this your son, we pray you."

"Is that all?" asked Montana.

"If you will wait there a little longer, I'll kneel and pray with you, my dear lad," said the bishop.

"No," answered the Kid, rising; "the floor's hard and my knees are soft. Where shall I find Pascual?"

"Somewhere along the street, watching the procession, I suppose," said the bishop. "His heart is not half a step away from the heart of a child. Perhaps that is why he is such a foolish man and such a good one."

"Tell me about him," begged Montana. "There's a fellow I want to know more about."

But just then he heard, out of the singing and the laughing and the shouting and the aimless chattering of the crowd in the street, the voice of one girl singing above the rest.

The sweetness of it ran into his soul even before his mind understood the meaning of the words.

She was singing:

> "*Love is not happiness.*
> *A horse under heel;*
> *A sword under hand;*
> *And red wine for the belly;*
> *But love is not happiness.*"

At that, he only paused to pull the mask again over his face before he leaned from the window of the bishop's palace and sent his voice ringing down in the second verse of that old Spanish song:

> "*Love is not happiness.*
> *Seeing is longing ;*
> *Winning is doubting ;*
> *Leaving is sorrow ;*
> *But love is not happiness.*"

"My son, is it proper that love songs should come out of the window of a clergyman?" said the bishop. But he was laughing till he remembered another thing: "And the whole town filled with Rurales and soldiers ready to seize you, El Keed! But I'll show you a back stairs to take you out behind the house——"

"With such a new blessing, how could I come into old trouble?" asked Montana. "Besides, she's answering me—she's waiting there in the street for me—that beautiful, laughing, singing, dancing devil, that traitor, Rosita."

He was fleeing from the room as he spoke. The bishop heard the feet thump hardly three times on the stairs, and then he saw the bounding figure issue out into the crowd.

CHAPTER XXIII

THE bishop, as he leaned from the window, saw the carriage of General Estrada, drawn by four horses, ploughing through the crowd, which scattered rapidly back on either hand, because on the back of the near leader of the team there rode a cruel devil with a blacksnake, and he knew exactly how to flog people out of his way. It was said that he could snip a bit off the flange of an ear, or nick a cruel little portion out of the back of a neck or take a portion out of the white cotton trousers of a peon with a cracking lash of his whip. This postilion would not have changed places with any man in the world. He looked about him with the leisurely eye of absolute power, at the present moment, rejoicing in the way the crowd felt his presence and fled from it.

Lolling back in the carriage was the general himself, leaning one hand on the hilt of a great, gilded sword and smoking one of his big cigars. Passing the palace of the bishop, he stood up, enormous in his carriage, spreading his feet to keep his balance against the jolting, and slowly, deliberately saluted.

The bishop, shocked by that insolence, drew back from the window a little and raised his eyes to that starry heaven which permits so many monsters to stalk the earth in triumph. Then he took out of his pouch at his girdle a folded paper which he opened and read by the dim flicker of the candles easily and swiftly, because it was a document which he had scanned more than once before.

It announced in great letters, at the top, a reward of ten thousand pesos for the apprehension of a man, dead or alive!

Ten thousand pesos—in this country where a thousand would seem a great fortune to many a starved, lean, dangerous mountaineer—men who shot straight because they could not afford to waste ammunition!

An American who speaks like a native Mexican.
He has darkened his skin with a stain.
He has black hair, but his eyes are blue.
He is tall, with wide shoulders.
His ways are graceful, his movements are slow.
He smiles very often.
He will come to a pretty woman as a wild horse comes
    to water.
Look for tall, handsome men with blue eyes.
Ten thousand pesos reward.
El Keed—dead or alive—El Keed.

That was the last line of the poster, in the largest lettering of all.

The bishop dropped the paper to the floor and leaned from his window again, breathless. He should have told the gringo about that published notice. But why should he tell such news to a man who surely knew all about what was happening.

And now he was down there in the crowd! Yes, through the swaying crowd the bishop himself could make out the man by his greater height and by a certain air that clung to him. And if he, with dim eyes and from a distance, could distinguish the prey in the throng, why did not those about him know the man instantly?

Because the eyes of the bishop had been opened, and the eyes of the crowd were closed by the brazen daring of the American. We see not the truth, but only that face of it which we expect to discover. And the last thing the men of Duraya expected was to find El Keed among them so soon after the foray upon the fort.

The carriage of the governor stopped not far ahead of the place where El Keed was moving through the throng. The governor himself stepped down. He approached a girl who was singing with a guitar. That was the daughter of the one-legged Miguel Santos. Her voice it had been, then, that had snatched El Keed out of the room. And still her singing was rising through the babel of the crowd, the sweetness of it cleaving like the glimmer of fire through smoke.

There stood the governor, holding out a hand to her, gesturing towards his carriage.

Hot anger stood up in the heart of the bishop, and then he saw that the girl was refusing. She was shaking her head. She was still singing her song:

> "*Love is not happiness.*
> *Seeing is longing;*
> *Winning is doubting;*
> *Leaving is sorrow . . .*"

The governor, turning suddenly, strode back into his carriage and flung himself back into his former seat, and all the crowd thronged about him and cheered his defeat.

The bishop was agape. He could not believe the thing that he had seen. The girl of the *cantina*—she had refused the governor; she had refused to be lifted suddenly into that dizzy place of honour; she had preferred her song?

"I have lived too much in this little room," said the bishop to his great heart. "How little I know of the goodness of my people!"

In the meantime, the rage of the governor at this public thwarting had come to a white heat. The others of the crowd could see the girl refuse the immense honour he offered, to make her the queen of the festival by placing her at his side in the carriage, the humbling of Ignacio Estrada by making such an offer to a girl in the street—but none of them could have heard the murmur which she placed between two lines of her song.

"Blood-drinker! Man-eating swine!"

She had said it for his ear only, and still smiling.

The madness that entered his brain kept it whirling like black smoke.

And straightway some of his fury seemed to enter the heart of the postilion, who thereupon fed the nearest of the crowd his whip. A few loud yells and screams told how the crowd scattered as the horses lunged forward again. All down the street ahead of the team spread confusion, and behind the carriage the crowd closed in again with a rapid clacking of tongues, monotonous streams of sound that poured curses on the head of the General Estrada and damned his ancestors and prescribed the future place of his abode.

But through the crowd that came laughing around the girl, congratulating her, wondering over her, the taller figure of the Kid stepped with a singular ease. He never seemed to jostle man or woman, but, as though he knew magic spots where his feet should rest, he glided through the press and came to her.

There was something about this man, dressed like themselves, masked like themselves, that made the other youths lose heart, and they gave back a trifle from around him as though they wanted to hear him and see him better.

For he had begun to sing in a good, rich, ringing

baritone, that fantastic old Castillian song, "Weave Me a Mantle." With the very first strains, the girl struck up the accompaniment on her guitar and gave the song her own voice, so that they walked on slowly, surrounded by their own music as with a wall of quiet, leaning their heads a little to one another.

And the words of the song could be translated like this:

> *Gather the starlight*
> *And weave me a mantle.*
> *Dip it in evening blue.*
> *Weave me a mantle ;*
> *Fringe it with moonshine*
> *And weave me a mantle*
> *To walk with my love.*

So long as the song continued, the crowd kept its distance, moving slowly with the slow pace of the singers, but as the song ended the tide of the festival rushed over the place and the level-streaming heads began to bob irregularly up and down again.

So, in a moment, the girl and Montana were more alone, more private in that crowd, than they would have been in the most secret of gardens.

She caught at his arm so that she walked close to his side, but she said, with her face upturned to him:

"If you knew me—if you knew what I have done——"

"I saw Estrada pull his hat over his eyes."

"But before—long before—there is a thing I have done——"

"Look!" said the Kid.

He held a gold piece in his hand.

"This is the past," said he. "Watch it!"

And he tossed the coin high over his head, so that it winked in the light of the lanterns.

She, over her shoulder, saw the gold flicker, arch up, fall. And the slim hands of a girl flashed up and caught it.

Rosita laughed. She had no envy for that lucky finder!

"That's the past—and let it go!" said Montana.

"Do you know?" she asked.

"Enough to make it worth the forgetting," said Montana.

"Governors come and governors go, but Montana rides for ever," said the girl.

> "*Weave me a mantle ;*
> *Fringe it with moonshine——*"

he sang.

They began to laugh together until he cried out:

"There's Brother Pascual grinning his big grin over the heads of the people! What a man that is, Rosita! Let's go to him, because he can tell me about Rubriz——"

She made the Kid pause.

"You don't know about Rubriz?" she gasped.

She began to read his face from side to side, up and down, as though somewhere in it she must find the knowledge.

"I don't know. What is it?"

"God forgive me!" cried the girl. "I can't tell you. No one dares to speak of it, but everyone knows—— Brother Pascual—he can tell you."

"Rubriz?" said Montana. "Has something happened to him? Mateo?"

He looked down at the agony in the eyes of the girl and then he went rapidly, cutting through the crowd by strength and adroitness, drawing the girl through the easy safety of his wake.

When he came up to the friar he said two words at the shoulder of the giant, whose eyes were so filled with the noise and laughter of the crowd that they overflowed with a sort of blind brightness. Every honest happiness that came to his fellow men was as two happinesses to that good fellow.

But at the voice of Montana he turned suddenly and threw up his hand as though to defend himself from an attack. Afterwards he crushed the wrist of the Kid with a terrible grasp.

"El Keed!" he whispered.

"Be quiet—people are staring, brother," cautioned the girl.

"Rubriz—tell me about Mateo!" urged Montana.

Behind the town, in that little sandy hollow where Montana had left the red mare, the three stood while Brother Pascual told to Montana a tale that curdled his blood.

Not everything was known. Men only knew how the great Rubriz had fallen to numbers and chance; how he had lain in the hands of the governor for a single day; and how he had been brought out of the fort during the middle of the next night a changed, perhaps a ruined, man. He had been placed in a carriage. Few had seen. But there had been a glimpse of a limply sagging form, arms and legs over which there was no control, the head hanging weakly over to the side.

Like a body newly dead, except that the eyes were living.

That was how the girl repeated words she had heard. And then the closed carriage had sped away on the southern trail.

"Where?" groaned Montana. "Where could they have taken him? What have they done with him, Pascual?"

"They have taken him where I am going to follow," said the friar, quietly, "but where it would be foolish for you to go, *amigo*. Foolish for me, also, but since Rubriz is dying for the sake of the church, I must go to join him."

"Dying?" echoed Montana.

"Don't you see?" put in the girl. "There's only one place that a devil like Estrada would send him. To the Valley of the Dead."

The name came over Montana like a horrible nightmare out of an almost forgotten sleep. He had heard of it before. All men in Mexico had heard of it, but it was a thing not to be whispered, not to be thought.

"We go together!" said Montana. But he hardly heard his own voice or believed that he had spoken.

"Pascual!" moaned the girl. "I told you what he would say! I told you that he would go. And I shall go also, then!"

"Hush!" said the friar. "You are a child. And what could you do?"

CHAPTER XXIV

THEY went south through the mountains, over the green plains, into a stricken land where running water was no longer found. Instead, there were standing pools or "tanks" of water that were foul with scum, filled with twisting, jerking forms of insect life. They had to dig shallow trenches a yard from the margin of these stink-holes and let the water seep in, purified a little by the filter through which it had run. But even when it had been strained in this slow and careful manner, that water would grow unbearably foul in half a day's ride under the southern sun.

It was the sun that possessed the world, and no one who had journeyed through that country could love the great bright disk again, not even if he found himself again in the cold north where it is a friend. Here it filled the entire sky with intolerable light and it blazed up again from the pale soil and the hot rocks.

Even the cactus was burned brown at the edges and all the thorns were black, tempered iron. The only other growth lay on the ground like grey smoke. There was no life for the eye and there was no sound for the ear. All was furnace by day, and, in the night, a black pit with the stars burning thin and far away through the dusty air. They had the feeling that they were not on a surface, but inside something.

After a day or two, not even Montana was capable of much speech and the songs with which he had cheered the first part of the journey ended. A man cannot sing with a dry throat and with cracking lips.

The greater part of the speech came from the friar. For every evening he prayed aloud for Rubriz, for El Keed, for all suffering mortals, and last of all he asked the mercy of God for himself.

In the morning he had a set speech in which he pointed out to Montana that they were not bent on a mission where success could be hoped for. For himself there was duty and an oath to lead him. What was there for Montana?

"There is a friend waiting," said Montana, finally.

And after the morning in which he made that answer, Brother Pascual gave up the daily entreaty.

They kept doggedly to the trail. It would have been possible to go down towards the coast and find better roads, but along those roads might be travelling men who had seen the published notice of a ten-thousand-peso reward for a tall man with black hair and blue eyes. So they had to keep to the terrible back country.

For Pascual there was a short-legged mule—because only short legs, he used to say, could possibly endure the strain of his weight. For the Kid there was the red mare, Sally. And they led with them the towering black stallion. Neither of them ever mounted the big horse, but each felt that it would be a sacrilege to ride the horse of a man who might be dead—who was surely in agony.

One night, when they were far south, Montana asked a few direct questions.

"Pascual," he said, "tell me in brief—not about the ghostly part of it or the legend—but what is the fact about the Valley of the Dead."

The friar pointed to the land.

"It is a bad place," he said. "But when water comes on the sand, anything will grow. Well, there is one valley where water flows and that valley was bought by two men—bought for nothing. They took labourers to the place. They planted tobacco. Never was such tobacco seen. It grew as weeds grow. It grew up out of the sand by magic. But some of the men who tended it grew ill. Others ran away. The sun addled the brain, it was so strong, and all about them was the ugly desert."

Here the friar paused and stood up and surveyed the flat horizon. He sat down again and went on:

"What was to be done? Tobacco meant money. Beautiful tobacco would grow in that valley, but there were no men to cultivate it. As fast as the labour was brought in the men would run away again. The desert was a terrible thing to cross. But anything was better than the valley. So the men who owned the valley thought of a plan. They went to the government. They said: 'Why do you spend much money on your prisons? Give us the evil-doers. We will take such care of them that they will never be seen again. And instead of charging money for keeping them, as your prisons do, we will pay you a little bit for every man. Yes, and even a little for the women.'"

"True!" muttered the Kid. "There are women in the valley. I'd forgotten that. So the government began to ship down the criminals—the murderers, and that sort of thing, eh?"

"At first, yes; but after a while there were not enough murderers. Then the men in the valley—and particularly Señor Juan-Silva—began to offer more money a head. They would send for a whole jailful of prisoners: Some were vagrants; some were petty thieves; some had disturbed the peace. One had been drunk; one was accused of being a revolutionist. And all of them were sent to die together in the Valley of the Dead. That is why the tobacco grows there so beautifully and Señor

Juan-Silva grows richer each year. It is he who owns the entire valley, now."

"This Juan-Silva," said the Kid. "What sort of a man is he?"

"They tell me that he is not a man."

"A devil, then?"

"If it were not for him, then the valley would be closed. Who but Juan-Silva would want to live there while the hundreds and the thousands die around him?"

"What does he use for guard?" asked Montana.

"Only Indians. They are willing to work there, happily, because they love to see the Mexicans die. They are well paid. They are the hunting-dogs—they are the pack which Juan-Silva loves to keep around him— these men, and a few others who are outcasts who cannot be taken back into their old places among them. They are the links between the inside of the valley and the outside—scoundrels who can afford to see their fellows dying around them!"

"Hai!" said the Kid. "This Juan-Silva, as you call him—this centre of the entire system—he's the sort of a fellow that I'd like to see."

"Yes," said the friar, "he is a man to see—and to forget. He is a man beyond prayers, I should say, my brother."

Then they came upon sight of the valley.

They had toiled all the day up a gradual slope and they came before evening to the edge of the highest plateau. Before them they saw the landscape descending in step beyond step beyond step into a dimness of sand dust and sun mist, and beyond the dimness the landscape rose again, in step beyond step beyond step.

After a time, by a change of the wind or of the light —or perhaps their eyes were a little more accustomed to peering into the strange mist—it seemed that the bottom of the view cleared out, as sediment clears out of water. And now they could make out, distinctly, a faint sheen of dull, purplish, dusty green in the bottom valley of all. It was not like a valley. It was like a great trench which had been hollowed out and out and out until no breath of wind could ever stir in it, and only the focused and refocused and accumulated sun was hoarded there in masses of infinite heat.

Already, at the top of the plateau where the travellers were pausing, the sun was hotter than even Montana had ever felt it before. It scalded his shoulders through the thick of his shirt; it gathered like a weight between the crown of the hat and his head. He could feel the air he breathed, hot and thick, until it was deep in his lungs. And the sweat ran out on his body and dried away instantly to salt! He could see the beads of water start to run down the face of the friar and disappear.

What would it be like, then, in the valley at the bottom of the slope!

The valley began in a jumble of high rocks and ran out again through a deeply carved badlands.

"Why would God put such a place on earth?" he could not help exclaiming, and the poor friar merely looked up, with both hands held in question to Heaven.

As for escape, he could understand why even the most desperate men would not be able to escape from the valley. The reason was that the mounted Indians guarded the verges of the pit of hell, and inside the pit there were other trained bloodhounds, and finally, the prisoners were kept chained day and night.

"Once inside, we'll never come out again," said Montana.

"Never again," said the friar. "And there is nothing

to draw you forward, but for a man like me, who has renounced the world——"

"Renounced my foot!" said the Kid. "Where's the fellow who gets more fun out of the world or loves the people of it more than you do?"

"Well," muttered Brother Pascual, "I have to go forward——"

And the Kid responded, sighing, "So must I!"

But he had a terrible sinking of the heart that told him only shame was driving him now, and that if the friar had not been in his company, he would have turned back and taken the lean red mare back across the horrible steppes towards the world of the living.

They went down towards the lower entrance to the valley until from a high place they could see the road that wandered away into the world. Up that road, the rumour said, the caravans of the damned were brought until they came to the lower foot of the Valley of the Dead. And here guards came out from the valley, the trusted agents of Juan-Silva, to pay down the head money and take charge of the chained criminals, and march them back into the valley.

There Brother Pascual made his evening prayer while big Montana looked through a powerful glass and saw three horsemen riding around the lip of the Valley of the Dead, and well behind them another trio, and behind these another set of three. The sun gleamed on their flesh. They were half-naked Indians. The sun burned in bits of flame on their lance-heads. He could see the little rounds of their shields.

"What's he done?" asked Montana. "Brought in the Indians and kept them wild?"

"Ay," said Pascual. "Even to the bows and the arrows. Men who try to run away die stuck as full of arrows as a porcupine is full of quills."

"I see," muttered Montana.

For his mind was struggling forward, striving to envisage the nature of this man who ruled the Valley of the Dead.

At least the creature was a king, even though he was a king of the damned.

The night fell suddenly. They made a fire no bigger than the cup of doubled hands would hold and over it they prepared their meal. They were in the midst of this when the mare ran suddenly in towards them and shouldered against her master. She stood with her head thrown up high, pointing like a hunting-dog at some danger that stalked them through the night.

"They're coming!" said Montana. "The damned Indians, it must be."

"Ay," said the friar calmly, "it must be they."

CHAPTER XXV

Of course they could not wait by the fire. They faded into the darkness at the right—and the mare stalked with them, bending her knees, fanning out her nostrils as she snuffed at the air out of which she had read her message.

For all the keenness of the eye of Montana, it was the friar who saw the outline first. He touched the shoulder of his friend.

"There!" he whispered, and raised the great beam of his arm.

And then Montana was able to see one dim, one single silhouette.

"It's only a single scout!" murmured Montana. "Hold the horse here, and I'll see if I can get him; he can tell us where the others may be——"

He turned himself into a big cat and slunk forward over the ground, moving in a swift semicircle, drawing up on that single rider. He was so close now that even if he were seen, he would be able to shoot straight. Now he was close enough to make the distance with one step and leap, and take the man captive, living. Beware of quick knife-work, however, when he was in close. This figure in the thick black of the night seemed small, almost fragile, but an ounce of Indian is often worth a pound of other flesh when it comes to hand-to-hand fighting.

Quartering from the rear, he came in on that silhouette—then a step and a leap brought him right on the back of the little mustang with the crushing strength of his arms cast around the body—of a woman!

The mustang reared, ready to pitch, and Montana slid off with a twisting, gasping, fighting figure in his grasp, and the big friar coming up at the run to help.

"Be still!" said Montana, through his teeth. "I'll do you no harm if——"

"Montana!" said the voice of Rosita.

His arms fell away from her. He was so stunned that the darkness moved before his eyes and the little dim stars in the zenith whirled around above his head. He could hear the friar exclaiming over her. He went in with the two of them towards the camp, but still he would not let his brain understand, for something inside him kept saying that it could not be. No woman who had seen the Valley of the Dead could willingly come closer than the first glance into the depths of it. And yet this was she, this was her voice.

Now she was sitting crosslegged by the fire, and the friar was giving her food, and she was eating, and lifting her eyes to the pain-struck face of Brother Pascual.

She looked thinner and older a little; her eyes were larger than they had been. She was quiet. All the bubble and the flash had gone from her. She looked like some product of the desert—brown and slender as a deer, with a sense of lightness, as though she could be away from this place in a flash.

Pascual was still pouring forth his gentle words, telling her of the danger here, and that she must start back at once towards a Christian land.

"Here," he said, "you are already on the lip of the Valley of the Dead!"

"Why do you talk to me, Brother?" she asked him, suddenly. "I am here on the lip of the cup—and you two will soon be inside it!"

Then said Montana, angrily, "What could you do, Rosita?"

"I could be here," she answered.

"But being here—what can you do to help?"

"I can keep the horses when you're inside—hell," said the girl. "They'd wander and starve. They'd be useless before you got out, and whether you bring Rubriz or only yourselves, or only one of you, you'll have to have horseflesh to carry you away from the Indians of Juan-Silva."

There was so much sense in this that Montana could only stare. Brother Pascual could do no more than stare, also, and at this the girl sat up and smiled at him. Suddenly Montana was aware that he never had seen her before so long unsmiling.

She sang to them in a voice not much bigger than a whisper:

> "*I come to the brown breast,*
> *I come to the desert,*
> *I come to my mother.*
> *Let others traverse her*
> *And wings fly over,*
> *But leave me there lost*
> *In the desert, my mother.*"

It was an Indian song. There was Indian in the girl, too. There was an infinity of strangeness behind the pretty face which had smiled so much for the drinkers in the *cantina* at Duraya. The heart and the mind of the Kid began to widen and widen as he looked at her now.

"That's the meaning, is it?" he asked her. "All the way across the desert you were not afraid?"

"I marked all your camping-spots. Where you had dug the trench I could find the water. I had an easy way, *amigo*."

"I wonder over you, child," said the friar.

"Why do you wonder?" asked the girl. "Has he told you that I sold him to General Estrada? Has he told you that?"

If there were Indian in the girl, there was Indian in the friar, also. He showed it now because he opened his mouth in astonishment and put his hand over the gap like any red man.

"Ten thousand pesos—dead or alive—El Keed—dead or alive—a tall man who smiles a great deal, with blue eyes and black hair. His ways are graceful—and he smiles a great deal! *I* sold him, Brother Pascual. I sold him to a dog—I sold him to Estrada!"

The Kid stood up.

"Don't come near me—don't forgive me!" she gasped.

And she went on in a sort of soft chant:

"I was going to be a great lady with a carriage and ten servants. I'd have rings and bracelets and necklaces. And I sold El Keed to get them. What is the hell for traitors, Brother Pascual?"

The tears began to roll down her face. The Kid sat down beside her and dried the tears with a bandana.

"Look," said the friar. "He forgives you."

"All men are fools," answered the girl. She put her head back on the shoulder of the Kid and looked up at him from under wet lashes. "Dying would do no good," she said to him. "What's the death of a creature like me? How would it help El Keed?"

"There is no mountain," exclaimed the friar, lifting his hands, "that repentance will not move."

"Ay," said the girl. "Go away from me, and take El Keed away, so that I can repent. I'm not repenting now."

"Ah, child," said the simple Pascual, "you must repent!"

"Have I two hearts?" she answered. "At one moment can I repent and love him, too?"

"Shall I go away?" asked the friar.

"Why should you?" she asked. "Do you think that I'm ashamed of *this*? I was never so much—in church!"

This idea of hers made her begin to laugh. She sat up away from Montana and began to shake her head.

"You two have done your poor cooking. But I have jerked venison, and two canteens of *fresh* water. Cool water, because I kept the sacking wet around them. Now *I* shall cook for you, and you shall see the difference. Also, I have one little flask of good brandy. You have to eat and to drink, because to-morrow——"

CHAPTER XXVI

In the dawn of the next morning they saw the dust cloud coming up the road, and before morning was far advanced they had sight of the caravan of the damned who were marching towards the Valley of the Dead. There must have been forty men, and perhaps ten or a dozen women, with a long cattle chain running from one to one, looped around the necks. The drivers went up and down the line. Three of them, with whips and guns, guarded the condemned, and in addition there was a rear guard of half a dozen Rurales.

At the same time, there came out of the lower mouth of the Valley of the Dead a pair of men naked to the waist, in short, wide-flaring trousers, with red sashes about their hips. They had on their heads straw sombreros with great brims broader than their shoulders. But, even so, those shoulders were sun-blackened. Their legs were bare from the knee to the sandals they wore. They were not Indians. They must, therefore, be a pair of the precious devils incarnate who superintended, for Juan-Silva, the immediate affairs of his hell.

They sat on their heels and smoked, not cigarettes, but fat cigars as they watched the caravan approach.

And as the poor wretches saw the entrance to their hell on earth and the two attendant demons who squatted beside it, such a voice came up out of them as made the air shudder.

One of the women fell. Her fall drew the loop of the chain strangulation tight about her throat and also nearly choked the men who had been marching before her and behind.

Two of the whip-wielders were instantly on the spot. They did not waste their time and their strength lifting her to her feet. Instead, they stood back, wielded their long lashes. The blood came out of her body. Montana could see it.

He buckled his chin down against his breast and squinted his eyes shut.

"Devils, devils," he screamed. But his scream was no louder than a whisper.

The poor friar, at the same spectacle, covered his face with his hands and fell on his knees.

Only the girl, with her face unmoved as stone, remained standing behind the fringe of great boulders that shielded them from view and yet gave them loopholes through which to view the procession and the entrance to the valley.

Once Rosita turned her head and looked curiously at Montana, a long, long glance. Whatever emotion she may have felt, that long side glance was the only evidence she gave of trouble in her mind or her nerves.

The woman who had fallen, got up from the beating and began to scream with her head fallen back on her shoulders; and that was the way she walked on, screeching at the sky, her head bobbing up and down with every step.

The friar was praying. Montana beat the knuckles of his fist hard and fast against his forehead. Only the girl looked on with calm, wide eyes.

The Kid saw her, at last. And a sort of horror, superior to that which had overcome him, now straightened him up. He went to the girl and said:

"Rosita, is there anything under the sky that you really give a damn about?"

She drifted her eyes over his face. She took out a good, clean white handkerchief and wiped away the sweat that was coursing over his skin.

"About you," she said. "I used to care about being a great, rich lady one day. Now I only care about you. All of you. Are you loathing me, Montana?"

"We won't talk," said the Kid.

"You want me to do more than you and Pascual when I see a woman beaten," said the girl. "You want me to shudder and fall in a faint. But look!" She tapped her fingers against the rock before them, a huge, sun-cracked boulder. "I am harder than that," said Rosita, and smiled at him.

For the first time she had spoken words that he could believe utterly. And yet, instead of wishing her away, he felt only a guilty sense of joy. Hard stone and hard steel—great things can be built with them.

When the caravan of the condemned had reached the mouth of the valley, the mounted guard from the rear came forward and an officer of the Rurales delivered to one of the two men from the valley a long paper, which the other then read over, checking off a list of names, apparently.

After that he walked around the line. A fat man he prodded in the ribs, and laughed. When he came to the woman who had fallen, he shrugged his shoulders and made a gesture of tossing something over his shoulder.

Having completed his inspection, he took from his belt a wallet, out of which he slowly counted shining pieces of money. When he had finished, the Rural recounted the cash and burst out in protest. The man of the valley argued with fewer words but heavier ones, it seemed. And presently the debate had ended. The

Rurales and the three whip-guards turned their horses and went down the road at a trot, soon lost behind the dust of their own raising.

The two men from the valley, in the meantime, examined the string of prisoners again. And when one of them came to the same unlucky woman who had fallen in the grip of the chain, he struck her suddenly behind the knees and sent her down with. a short, strangled screech.

The Kid drew a gun, but the girl beside him caught his hand.

They were kicking the woman to her feet again, laughing. Then, with a shouted command, they started the string of the condemned forward into the throat of the valley. But the two guards did not follow immediately. They seemed to realize that whatever the lips of the valley closed over would never pass through them again. They remained to argue heatedly over some money which one of the rascals held in his fist. Perhaps it was the overplus out of which the officer of the Rurales had been cheated.

But Montana, as he watched, saw a chance for action stranger than anything he had ever dreamed of before. He looked at the friar, still lost in profound prayer. He looked quizzically at the girl; then he started down the slope behind the rocks, swerving quickly from one to another until he was very close to the spot where the two still argued.

They were not men. They had the faces of beasts. The evil that was in them made them seem like two bloody brothers. And now with snarling mouths and reddened eyes they threatened each other.

They were still at it when the Kid stepped out from behind the nearest boulder.

"There's a better way, brothers," he said.

They started and faced him with one movement. Both were armed, but only with knives, and that long-barrelled Colt in the hand of Montana, held no higher than his hip, watched them both with a single eye of darkness.

"I've been hearing," said Montana, "that only choice men can get work in the Valley of the Dead, my friends, and because I want to take a look at the place, I've decided to make a vacancy. Which one of you ought to die?"

They stared at him; they stared at the gun.

"You, there," directed Montana, "you with the frog face, pick up that length of rope and tie it to the wrist of your partner."

The thing was done.

"Now, you on the right, tie the other end of that rope to your *compañero.*"

The man obeyed.

"The pair of you have knives," said Montana. "I sit here as the judge. God knows that there's nothing so useful you can do as die. The winner lives, then, and I step into the sandals of the other rat. Start! You understand? Or do you want me to sift some lead into your hides?"

The smaller of the two seemed to take in the idea first. His knife came out in a flash as he said:

"A gift for you, Felipe!"

And he struck the blade into his companion. There was weight enough in the blow and it was well enough aimed, below the left shoulder; but with a light, tinkling sound the blade snapped in two. The point, no doubt, had struck a rib bone.

"Francisco!" screamed Felipe. "Devil!"

And he hurled himself right at the other.

Felipe had the strength, the length of arm, and a

knife which was unbroken. He had the relentless vigour of a bulldog, too. But Francisco was as wily as a snake. He could not run, because of the rope that tied him to his companion. But he could use that rope to jerk Felipe off balance.

A long slash had ripped open the breast of Francisco. But he had wit enough to spring far to the left and throw his body to the ground. Felipe toppled after him, met in falling by the up-jabbing knife fragment in the hand of his fellow.

They rolled together like two tomcats.

The fight was as brief. Big Felipe lay on his back, his throat well opened, a dozen other jagged wounds in his breast from the rapid knifework of Francisco, and Francisco, pouring blood, dragged himself up and sat on the body of the dead man.

He untied the rope from his left wrist.

"Well," said Francisco, "I am done for; but that doesn't matter. I sit on the big half-wit now, and I'll still be his master in hell. If only the señor could see how I sit now! If you really see Juan-Silva, *amigo*, tell him how I won the fight—and with a broken knife."

He put his hands over the pouring wounds in his breast. The blood still leaked out around his fingers. He extended his hands before his face and laughed.

"This is the strange thing," he said. "The pain is all in the skin, not in the heart. I tell you, friend, that if people knew how easy it is, they would as soon die as drink coffee for breakfast. And if——"

Here he choked suddenly.

He bowed his head and leaned his hand on the shoulder of Felipe.

After a moment he said:

181

"I'll be choking—in a minute—and kicking like a chicken with its head off, I suppose. But that'll soon be over."

The strength went out of him. The arm which supported him began to shake violently.

"Who are you?" he breathed.

"El Keed," said the Kid.

The head of Francisco jerked back. There was a loose-lipped, gibbering laughter in his face for a moment.

"So!" he said. "And a great man knows how Francisco died."

Gradually he sank down. That choking and kicking which he dreaded did not come to Francisco. His body rolled away from Felipe a half turn and he lay still. One breath more puffed the dust up around his head. He shuddered. And that was the end.

Montana untied the bloody rope from the wrist of Felipe and threw the dripping thing over the rocks. Big Brother Pascual was running frantically down the hillside. The girl sat on a sun-bleached stone and looked calmly on the dead.

It was she who explained when poor Pascual was gaping and stammering at the slaughter.

"You see, brother? These fools killed each other. No one inside the valley will ever know that Montana made them fight. And you—a poor priest driven out of the world because of many sins—why, you've often told me that you are full of sin, Pascual!"

"I am—I am!" stammered Pascual. "But what does *this* mean?"

"A way into the valley, don't you see?" said the girl. "Juan-Silva keeps so many guards inside his valley among his dead. So many, and no more. Usually he gets the new ones from among the prisoners, but this day two new ones walk into the valley. The poor friar who repents his sin and wants to find a living death, eh? And here's El Keed himself, driven through Mexico, hunted like a dog until he has to take shelter in the Valley of the Dead. Well, will Juan-Silva believe you both? Will he make guards of you? And even if he does, will that give you a chance to set Rubriz free? How can I tell? There is one chance in ten thousand—and that's a good chance for Montana to take!"

Brother Pascual said: "Friend, how has this happened?"

"Two mad dogs. They took each other by the throat. The rest of what Rosita says—well, it's true enough. You see our ghost of a chance, Pascual?"

"To walk in—freely—to give ourselves into the hands of Juan-Silva?" muttered the friar.

"Well," said Montana, "I don't know a better way. And somehow, I'd rather take the first chance and die with it than to wait there in the hills, looking down into hell from the brink. The longer a fellow looks at the jump, the harder it is to take, *amigo*."

He could not help adding:

"But why should two men go in, Pascual? Let me go alone. Whatever I can do, I'll try. And you wait out here—with Rosita—wait as many days as you have any hope—and then take her back to her people."

"I have no people," said the girl. "I have you. When you are gone, I have nothing. But you, Pascual, stay out here with me. If we can't talk, we can pray. I've always wanted to be taught how!"

Pascual put his heavy arm over the shoulders of Montana.

"Brother," he said, "let us go in."

"Rosita," said Montana, "there's no use talking to you—no use telling you that there's danger from Juan-Silva's wild devils of Indians. I know that. You'll wait out there for us with the horses. God bless you, Rosita!"

"He knows nothing about me," said the girl.

"Child! Child!" reproved the friar.

"Hush, and turn your head, Pascual," answered the girl. "I have to say good-bye to El Keed."

CHAPTER XXVII

THEY walked in together. Running water must have cut the twisting channel through the rock, but the river of the Valley of the Dead no longer flowed through the old outlet. It had found an exit underground at the base of the eastern cliff, what small part of the water was not used to irrigate the fields.

Not a hundred yards through that winding pass they came out upon view of the valley floor. It was flat as levelling could make it, and from the fields, black with new water, arose a great steam into the morning sun. That was part of the mist which from a distance obscured the floor of the valley.

They could see the caravan of the condemned going slowly up the road into the valley, and mounted men rode before them and behind. But it was strange that even the Valley of the Dead should be unguarded at the entrance.

Unguarded? As the two stepped into the road, a half-dozen mounted men sprang their horses out from angling crevices in the rocks. They came at the friar and Montana with frightful yells, ropes whirling over their heads. Such faces, grinning with such diabolic joy, the Kid had never seen, except for Felipe and Francisco, who now lay dead at the entrance to the valley. And a thunderclap of conviction struck him as he saw the friar with raised head calmly await the onrush. He had come into the valley with a fanatic, not a quick-witted helper. And probably they were lost together. At least, to resist would be perfect folly. So Montana stood fast with the friar, and three nooses whistled. He was caught about the arms at the elbows; about the body at the hips; about the neck by a rope that burned his throat as it was drawn taut.

The friar was snared in almost an equivalent fashion. And the leader of the party reined his Indian pony in front of the captives. He and his men were dressed exactly as Francisco and Felipe had been. The endless heat of the Valley of the Dead made more clothes folly. And always, in spite of the huge width of the sombreros, the bodies of the men were sun-blackened almost beyond belief.

This fellow was an elder whom time had withered. His hair was grey. His skin was powdered over in places with grey, also. And on a skeleton neck a skeleton head was placed, the hollow eyes glaring down at the Kid.

"How much fool are you, stranger?" he asked. "Or do you know what place this is?"

"Ask Francisco and Felipe how much fool I am," said the Kid.

"Francisco? Felipe? What do you know about them? And who's this man in the friar's gown?"

"Francisco and Felipe have just finished each other off with their knives. They're lying in the sand outside the mouth of the valley. And that makes room for two more good men in the valley, doesn't it? You see, friend, that we've come to take the vacant places."

"A good face but a hollow brain," said one of the guards.

"Go, look for Francisco and Felipe, Emilio;" said the commander of the guard. "The rest of you, bring the pair of them along. And mind you two—if one of you moves a single side-step, he'll be dragged the rest of the way by the neck. He may get to the house of Juan-Silva with a bit of breath in his lungs, but he'll be missing some skin off his body. You, there, friar, do you know what place you've entered?"

"The Valley of the Dead, I suppose it to be," said good Pascual.

"Well, why are you here?"

"He's going to raise them," suggested a guard. "He's going to raise the dead!"

They all laughed. They laughed heartily, rolling a little in their saddles.

"He'd better try to raise himself," said another. "What will Juan-Silva say?"

"It's a good net that the birds want to fly into."

The beating hoofs from the rear told that Emilio was overtaking them. And now he pulled up his horse at the side of the man of the death's-head.

"Francisco and Felipe—both dead—cut to pieces—their knives beside them. Hai! It's a thing to see. There's blood spread over half an acre. You wouldn't find so much blood in a pair of bulls."

The leader heard this report with a nod of the head.

"This is a thing that needs thinking," he said. "Even Juan-Silva will close his eyes and smile his smile when he hears about it."

They had come out, now, to the centre of the valley, with tobacco-fields on both sides of them, and Montana looked through the frightful sun-glare and the rising steam at the heights that receded step by step into the distance. It was like a vast theatre, with benches hewn out on which prodigious monsters could seat themselves. And from all sides the reflected heat poured into the cup of the valley and was held there. To breathe was difficult. In this short time the clothes of Montana had become soaking wet, and the huge friar was visibly soaking.

But Brother Pascual kept his head high and retained, always, that faint smile which went with him through life, as though he found something worthy of both pity and amusement in all that passed beneath his gaze. Never had Montana admired him as he admired him now. Only as Pascual saw the gangs of labourers in the fields did his smile go out and a great breath swell his chest.

For they were scattered here and there, long lines of miserable creatures, almost naked. For the women an abbreviated skirt afforded some decency. For the men there was a loin cloth. And for the men and women, both, there were the huge sun-hats which gave shelter from the killing strength of the sun. The swaying of the broad-bladed, short-handled hoes made irregular lines of light across the fields.

Labour in such a temperature as that? That, alone, was enough to justify the significant name of the Valley of the Dead. And here and there, behind the workers, went the overseers—each with a whip in his hand. More than once Montana saw a long lash curl back behind the shoulders of an overseer as he drove a laggard to swifter progress.

He could see more details as they drew closer, and above all the dragging weight of the chains that held every one of the condemned, day and night, for ever.

Two square-shouldered buildings stood in the centre of the valley. One for the women, said a guard, and another for the men.

"But there are hundreds in here—and how can they be crowded into places of that size?" asked Montana.

"By sleeping them in tiers five high," grinned the guard, "and where there isn't room to lie down, they stand."

The thing spread itself in a grisly picture before the

eyes of Montana—the thick of the gloom lighted by one or two dull lamps, and the groaning of the sick and the despairing, and the horrible steam and stench of close-packed humanity.

But somewhere within the walls of this valley was Mateo Rubriz. Perhaps his chains were jangling in one of the near-by rows of hoers as he drove the blade of his hoe inches deeper than the rest. And the thought of him transformed the place for the Kid. The strangeness of their past swept over him, and a feeling that there must be a future for them both.

They came, now, towards a building with a very long, low front.

"There's your master. There's Juan-Silva—and may God help you!" said one of the guard.

To which the captain answered, chuckling: "God can't look in here. The steam's too thick."

And once more they all laughed at this.

In front of the place they were halted. In place of the lariats, they were tied with short cords, even their feet being hobbled; afterwards, they were led through an entrance door down a naked hall, and so into the brightness of an open court.

Here sat Juan-Silva under an awning of the brightest old Mexican featherwork. He was cross-legged, like an Indian, on a mat of woven dyed grass, and he sat at the verge of a shallow run of water whose swift ripples threw upwards a continual play of reflected light on the face of the despot of the Valley of the Dead.

He wore, like the lowest of his labourers, only a loin-cloth, so that Montana could see the withered limbs and the sagging paunch of an old man of eighty, at least. His head was bald as an egg. It was strangely shaped, with a dividing crease in the centre between the big front and back lobes. From his face the spare flesh had been melted away by time, but the skin had not shrunk to a tight fit. Over the jowls, beside the mouth and hanging under the chin, were almost rigid folds of the old, tough hide.

He had once been a tall man with wide shoulders, and still he was not bowed, but the years had turned him into a mummy. And, as in a mummy of a young man, his sunken cheeks were drawn out lean and hard because he still possessed a full set of teeth. When he spoke, his lips first furled back over the teeth, which then parted before utterance came.

This curious contortion had the effect of a smile, at first, and afterwards it was as though he wanted to get his lips away, carefully, from teeth that might cut them. The voice itself was low-pitched and the vibrations could almost be counted. One might have called him a dying man, but Montana had the conviction that death would still be postponed for many years.

How did he manage to retain his place? Every year, according to rule, the tax inspectors, at least, journeyed into the Valley of the Dead, and every year they came out again without registering a claim against the monstrous rule of this evil old man. Well, money can close most mouths, even a little of it.

Juan-Silva was saying:

"Have we visitors? Have we really visitors at last? What do you mean, my friends, by tying up their hands and hobbling their feet? Is that treatment for a guest?"

The skeleton-headed captain of the guard—compared with Juan-Silva he looked like a young man—answered:

"They came into the Valley, señor, and so we brought them here safely. Francisco and Felipe, who went out to bring in the new gang of prisoners, have killed each other at the mouth of the valley—and these two say that they've come to take up the room that Francisco and Felipe have left."

It was a clear enough statement.   Juan-Silva pondered it for a moment.   Then he said:

"Take the friar into my own room and leave him there. Untie the ropes.   Let him be free.   Only watch—in case he should need anything.   I am glad that the Church is smiling on the Valley of the Dead.   But this other one, he is different.   Let me talk with him, my friends."

CHAPTER XXVIII

POOR Brother Pascual, when he knew that he was to be parted from his friend, cast one glance of longing towards Montana, and then went away surrounded by several of the guards. Others remained with the Kid. And he felt those amazingly young eyes, brighter than youth in the dead setting of that face, scanning him, probing at him.

"You have a name, señor?" asked Juan-Silva.

"Several," said the Kid, smiling. "Some people call me Arizona, and some call me Montana. And some simply call me El Keed. That is south, here, in Mexico."

He wondered, vaguely, if the knowledge of that name had penetrated as far as the Valley of the Dead, even? The death's-head who faced him showed no sign of recognition, but the others instantly shifted and stirred a little. At this, Juan-Silva lifted a bony finger and pointed to one.

"*You* know something," he said. "What is it you know?"

"A Rural told me," said the man. "One of the Rurales who were bringing up new prisoners to the valley entrance. He told me about El Keed."

"And he said?" went on the ancient man.

"He said, señor, that he would give the halo from his hope of sainthood and his good right hand, also, if only he could become the captor of El Keed."

"Tell me in one word—is there a price on the head of this man?"

192

"There is a price—ten thousand pesos—on the head of this gringo!"

This informant was a good, broad chunk of a man with the top of his nose bashed in, perhaps by the kick of a horse or a mule, and with his nostrils correspondingly flaring wide so that he always seemed to be out of breath, or in a passion.

"Ten thousand pesos?" said Juan-Silva. "Well, that is money, too!" He rubbed his lean hands together and Montana heard the chafing of the dry skin. "But ten thousand pesos, why, my friend? Is this a great man-killer and robber? This gringo? But is he really a gringo?"

"I am an American," admitted the Kid.

"I have known a few," said the rasping but subdued voice of Juan-Silva, "but I have never known any good to come out of them. Go on—you!—and tell me why they want to pay so much money for El Keed—dead or alive?"

"Yes, dead or alive. That is how the poster reads."

"Well, we have never made much money out of dead men, but we may begin to export them," said Juan-Silva.

He pushed out his tongue and ran it slowly over his lips, as though his mouth were sore and needed comfort.

"But you still have a story to tell."

"Why, this is the man," said the informant, "who has ridden from one end of Mexico to the other, with the Rurales trying to catch him and always missing, just missing, and leaving behind them a good many wounded and a good many dead and dying."

Juan-Silva looked straight at Montana.

"Have you killed some of the brave Rurales?" he asked.

"I have," said Montana.

"Ha! And you boast of it?" asked Juan-Silva.

193

Suddenly Montana felt that to this terrible old man it would be far wiser to tell most of the truth. Therefore he broke out, speaking truth from the bottom of his heart.

"I never saw a Rural I would not have put bullets through if I could!"

"Ah!" said Juan-Silva. "That's the truth of it, is it?" He began to nod his head, wagging it far up and down. At last he said: "I, also! I never have seen a Rural I did not wish dead!"

A look of wonder ran over the faces of the guards. They turned their heads ever so little towards one another. A glimmer of apprehension and relief came into their eyes. They had learned one new point in the endless riddle of their master's mind.

"And why have you wanted to ride through Mexico, up and down?" asked Juan-Silva.

"It is a great country, with plenty to see," said Montana. "And I have seen most of it!" he boasted.

"If you have seen it, why do you still come?"

"To see it all again, señor."

"And you are El Keed? Even I have heard of him," said Juan-Silva. "Now, tell me the truth and I think there'll be no harm for you here in the Valley of the Dead. Why did you come here?"

"Because ten thousand pesos are posted up for me."

"You were hunted, eh?"

"Every man in the mountains was cleaning his rifle. The *charros* were fixing their eyes for me. The shepherds, even, were whetting their knives."

"And at last they drove you in here for refuge?"

"I thought it was better to be a living man among the dead than a dead man among the living."

"Do you hear, my children?" said Juan-Silva. "This man is also witty. Very soon he will have me laughing. El Keed is known to be a pleasant fellow—and perhaps this is really El Keed. Think, then, if I catch in my hand, in one day, a friar and El Keed, walking together! But El Keed," he went on, "carries with him a magic pair of guns that never miss."

"Mine miss plenty of times," said Montana, frankly.

It was not heat that was making him sweat, now; it was the thought of joining those rows of chained labourers in the field.

"Set him free, foot and hand," commanded Juan-Silva.

This was done instantly. Juan-Silva dipped his hand and his withered arm into the water that ran before him and picked out one of the big, shining white pebbles. As soon as it was taken from the water the silver brilliance began to leave it.

"This is a bird. It takes wing. Shoot it, *amigo!*" said Juan-Silva, and tossed the stone into the air.

The gun flashed into the hand of the Kid, but he missed that best moment when the stone hangs a trifle at the top of the throw. He missed it there; he missed it as it gathered speed in the descent; but his third bullet turned the rock into a puff of white dust when it was just above the ground.

"Well," said Juan-Silva, canting his head critically to one side, "that is very good, but that is not El Keed. Try again!"

He picked up two stones and threw them very high and to a distance. The Kid, turning, found the terrible sun in his eyes. The stones were little black specks. One of them he knocked into nothingness at the top of its rise. The other he missed twice as it fell. He was half blind with the dazzle; he heard the stone fall on the gravel of that naked patio.

The sound was a voice to him. He heard a slight

murmur among the guards, and saw the flash of their malice.

"And that," said Juan-Silva, "was still worse. But all good things come in threes. So here you are again!"

Three flashing pebbles he threw, this time. The second gun was already in the hand of the Kid. With his scowling brows he made a shadow that enabled him to look close to the sun. He dared not miss, and therefore he held his fire a heart-taking instant before each shot. The first stone disappeared at the top of its rise, the second as it began to fall, and the third when it was a foot from the ground.

The guards drew in a gasping breath in unison. Juan-Silva said:

"That is very good. You are El Keed—I am almost sure. How can you make me quite certain, my friend?"

"Question me," said Montana.

"This man, this gringo, this famous Montana who has ridden through our Mexico and left dead men behind him, he is also a singer, eh? He sings the good songs, the old songs. I have heard about that, too. Will you sing for me, *amigo?*"

He leaned forward with his chin cupped in his hand, his elbow on his knee. And the Kid searched his memory eagerly. Then, after humming a note or two, he smiled and struck into that famous old stirring song of another age:

> "*Land and house, horse and saddle,*
> *Shield and lance, sword and dagger,*
> *Take them and I still am strong.*
>
> *Take the priest, take the friend,*
> *Take the wife, take the child,*
> *Leave only faith in my honour.*'

"Good," said the old man, closing his eyes as though the song were still running through his mind. "Very good, and now you are twice El Keed. Be it three times and we are friends. But as I said before, all right things are in threes. And, El Keed, I have heard, as a hunter is like a cat that sees in the dark. You shall have that chance, *amigo*. If you see in the dark, you are El Keed and no other. Besides, I shall give you a chance to do something that will be very famous, afterwards."

He pointed to the thin-faced captain of the guard.

"Take him to the room of the old mill. See that not a single ray of light is entering. The room is close. He will not want many clothes. Strip him to one garment. Since he loves our Mexico so well, he must love the machete of our peons, also. Give him a good one, a sharp one. Be fair with him, and afterwards call up three prisoners who are new in the valley. Big men, strong men, quick men. How should we try good steel except on tough, strong wood? Give each of the three a machete. Tell them El Keed will meet them in the dark of the room. Thrust them in to him. Feed them to this puma—this mountain lion. Tell them that if he dies they shall not be prisoners; they shall be guards."

In a dark room—armed with a heavy machete only—to encounter three bloodthirsty peons who had been raised to the use of that weapon—to struggle with three men who had something better than life to fight for?

The Kid turned a little towards old Juan-Silva, not to appeal, but to curse the unquenchable bloodthirst of the tiger. But Juan-Silva was already reclining on his mat, thrusting his legs out into the terrible heat of the sun and groaning with pleasure. He had closed his eyes. Already, perhaps, he had forgotten his last commands. Cursing and pleading alike would mean nothing to him.

So it was in silence that Montana moved away, surrounded by his guards.

The captain of them moved with a short gait, almost mincing his way like a dancing boy, and as he went he sang huskily:

> *"Land and house, horse and saddle,*
> *Shield and lance, sword and dagger,*
> *Take them and I still am strong."*

He kept on singing the song to the end, but a great laughter began to interrupt him and choke away his voice. The rest of the guards joined in the mirth, but softly, with a sound like the humming of a hive.

CHAPTER XXIX

THEY brought up three men from the fields.

Big Montana, in the meantime, was stripped and given a pair of the unbleached cotton shorts. He was given a machete, too, the heavy knife widening towards the point to make its stroke more effective in mowing down cane or rushes. He gripped it and weighed it. Among the natives, he knew, the science of machete play had been cultivated almost to the point of small-sword fencing. And he, for the first time in his life, was holding the weapon!

He looked over the three. They were all big. Vidal—Leon—Garcias—they were named to him by the captain of the guard, who chuckled as he spoke their names.

They were big, and the brute was written all over them. Not for minor offences had they been sent to the Valley of the Dead. And they had remained long enough in the place to have in their eyes contempt for death compared with their horror of the life they had been enduring. The marks of the chains were on their necks and ankles, now for the moment made free from weight. The bitter labour had rubbed away from their bodies all spare flesh. And each man knew machete-play. Each had in his eyes a light brighter than that which flickered over the keen edges of the knives, while they measured the Kid as a butcher measures a beef. In full daylight, any one of the three, he knew, would have been more than a match for him at this game.

But Juan-Silva preferred a hugger-mugger frightfulness in the dark. He would lie yonder on his mat and smile and taste his own cruelty in the back of his throat.

The grey-headed captain was saying:

"You three get in there. El Keed first. When the three of you are done for, El Keed will rap on the wall and we'll come in to see what's happened. Or if the three of you finish him, shout, and you're free from the chains. No more of the sleep-house, you hear me? No more of the spoiled beans and cabbage, but meat that a man can eat. Do you hear me tell you?"

Hear him? They grinned on one another, open-mouthed, and suddenly they joined hands, nodding. The Kid understood that gesture. They would remain linked together by the hands so that none of them might fall foul of another by mistake, in the darkness. They would have more than united defence—they would have the strength of companionship in the thick blackness.

"Go in first! El Keed first! This is El Keed, *amigos*. This is the gringo. If you have heard of him before, let Mexicans be able to forget about him to-day."

The door opened slowly, because it was a weight even with the hands of two men pulling at it, and as the light entered, the Kid walked into a big, round chamber that might have been a tank built to hold water. There was no feature of interest in its construction. On one side it was exactly as on another, except that the wall had been built up of great thickness only for some eight feet of its height, after which a lighter wall went up to the roof, leaving a deep shelf that ran all around the compartment.

"Now, *amigos!*" barked the voice of the grey-head, and as the great door closed, Montana looked behind him and saw, as the light pinched out, that the three were coming for him in a rush, their bare feet whispering on the stone floor.

He fled. The closing of the door left him in utter darkness. Then he turned and dropped to one knee, one hand, with the machete poised over his right shoulder.

But the whisper of the footfalls did not sweep straight up to him. They paused, a little to his left. Then silence followed. He could see nothing, but he thought that he could feel a pressure on his brain from their approach. Tip-toe, three cats in the dark, they could hunt him by scent, perhaps. They had looked near enough to the beast for that!

The thick of the dark was a weight, a steady weight. And he felt his eyeballs starting out of his head with strain.

Then he remembered that his eyes were useless. He might as well close his eyes, so he closed them. Sense of touch would have to serve him, completely.

But in the meantime, three stalking devils were moving through the darkness to find him, find him they must, sooner or later. Spread out in a line, they could not fail to make contact with him, and at the first touch three machetes would fall to work. He might strike down one of them, but the other two would be certain to bury the heavy, razor-sharp blades in him.

He could feel the pain—the nausea of it.

And if he fled, the noise of his feet would bring them all the more swiftly on him.

He rose and drew back, little by little. When he touched the wall, something went by him, breathing. It was barely audible, but the sound could be heard, nevertheless. The three of them had moved slowly by. It was like magic; three huge men could not pass in such a silence!

Loathing which was greater than fear was driving him now. But he told himself that there was time. It would be minutes before the line of the three returned to this same spot.

He reached behind him and gripped the edge of the stone shelf above him. He laid the machete on it, stepped a pace away from it, then freshened his grip on the ledge with both hands. Slowly—he must not make a sound—he muscled himself up. When his shoulders were level with his hands he swung a leg over the edge of the shelf and stretched himself out prone.

There must be no sound, but his lungs were bursting with the effort which he had just made. There seemed to be no oxygen in the hot, thick, stale air as he mastered his breathing. His whole body shook. The pangs of strangling made him gape his mouth wide open, but he fought back the panic until, little by little, drawing only small, quick, unwhispering breaths, he was almost normal again.

There was not room for his entire body to lie in any comfort and security. A part of his width projected, and when the searchers thought to feel along the ledge he would be found instantly.

That thought made him want to leap down at once, regardless of any tell-tale noise he would make. But the idea which had entered his mind sustained him. He kept his eyes closed. Three men in the dark, and as a blind man he must master them!

He began to work off the short trunks in which he was dressed. That required minutes and minutes—an endless time—heaving himself up on one elbow and his knees, working the cloth down towards the ankles, sharpening his ears so that not a sound could be heard without first coming to his own senses.

But at last he had the cloth in his hand.

He lay on his left shoulder, in his left hand holding the cloth to the extent of that arm. In his right hand he kept the machete. And then he waited, with eyes closed.

His left arm began to grow numb. If that happened, his plan was lost, for it depended on delicacy of touch. No stir of wind would move that hanging cloth. It was to Montana as the main spy-thread on which the spider keeps her foot for news of anything that touches her web.

Feeling was fast leaving his left arm. He kept flexing his left hand from time to time. And his eyes were closed. To attempt to see in utter night would only make him strike astray when the time came.

The cloth pulled slightly in his hand. He hesitated, perhaps for the thousandth part of a second, and then struck with all his might. Into bone the heavy blade clove. A dropping weight almost pulled the knife from his hand, but he wrenched it free.

"Diablo!" a man had gasped.

He reached far out and struck at the sound. The machete shore through flesh, gritted on bone.

And a man screamed, short and sharp.

"Vidal!—Garcias!—Christ!—he has seen in the dark! Vidal!"

"Vidal!" said another voice. Then "Vidal is gone— it was he that dropped——"

"My God, I am killed, Garcias!"

"Hush! Fool—fool—the noise——"

But already, under cover of those voices, Montana was down from the shelf.

His foot touched a warm liquid. He stepped softly away from the voices. He lay on the floor, stretched out flat, the machete gripped in his right hand over his head. The cool of the floor turned instantly hot with his body.

He was sweating all over, and the air was thicker and staler than ever. He had a frenzied second of thinking that it would be death by suffocation merely to remain in the room.

Then he took hold of himself and cast the panic away.

That man he had struck through the skull—that Vidal —he was dead; and another was badly wounded—Leon, that would be. There remained Garcias. Well, it was for Garcias that he lay stretched along the floor.

His mind stretched back to old Juan-Silva. Perhaps it would be better to die here, mangled with the strokes and the savage thrusts of a machete, than to go out to face that terrible old man again. All that he could think of was the stiff, hard folds of the dried skin, and the voice, like the sound of a death rattle.

A wild yell beat through the room; the echoes of it crowded back from the walls.

"I am dying! I die! Mercy in the name of God! Mercy in the name of God——!"

Hands began to beat on a wall.

"Give me light to die by! Give me one ray of light— light—light!"

The voice went up into a wordless screeching. It changed to a gasping, a choking sob.

Would they open the door when they heard the beating of those hands?

But Montana lay still and made every nerve in his body alert, for perhaps, under cover of the dying man's noise, that Garcias was stepping swiftly here and there through the darkness, searching. He was the hugest of the three, the most perfect animal.

Something cold touched the knee of the Kid. He struck with the full weight of his arm, three feet above the floor, and the blade went deeply home.

"*Dios!*" gasped an indrawn voice.

A blow fell; steel shattered on the stone floor inches from the head of the Kid. The sparks leaped, died, showed him nothing. He had torn his blade free and struck again, swinging sidewise. He found nothing. He leaped far forward and clove the air again, and again the blade chopped through soft flesh, jarred on bone.

Something fell heavily on the floor.

He stood on tiptoe, the machete poised.

He stood for terrible seconds, waiting; and then he heard a queer, bubbling groan.

That was all.

Behind him, Leon was silent at last.

He went to the wall and fumbled his way gradually around it. When, at last, he reached the inside of the door, he beat three great strokes on it with the butt of his machete.

The door quivered, opened a little.

A blasting ray of light struck through and almost blinded him.

"Who is it? Leon? Vidal? called the voice of the grey-headed captain.

"El Keed," said Montana.

They jerked the door wide open. The sight of him seemed to shock them like a blow. He looked down and saw that he was naked, and blood spattered and streaked him.

Blood was still running slowly down the length of the machete. It looked thin purple on the steel, and red as it gathered and fell from the point.

"Here," he said to the captain, offering the weapon. "I'm finished with it."

The captain, as a man stunned, took the weapon with an uncertain hand; and looking back over his shoulder, the Kid saw that Leon was still writhing a little; Vidal sat as though asleep, his head fallen down between his knees. But Garcias was raising himself slowly on his hands.

From the frightful sight of him Montana turned quickly away.

CHAPTER XXX

THE "good" treatment of the friar, when Juan-Silva had commended him to the keeping of his guards, consisted in taking him to a long, low shed, where he was promptly stripped of his robe and clad in the cotton trousers which were the universal garb in the valley. The chain was fitted to his ankles, the length of it running up to a steel collar that enclosed his neck, and as the blacksmith riveted it in place he laughed a good deal.

"A bigger neck was never fitted. Maybe the singing of psalms and chants has swelled it, brother, but a few days in the Valley of the Dead will make it shrink again."

Then they took him into the fields. With the wide straw sombrero to cover his head he was placed in a line of labourers. Absently he worked, swaying the wide-bladed hoe, and forging ahead so far beyond the others that they began to curse him, because the overseers, shouting, began to drive the rest to keep them up with this tremendous pace-maker.

When the poor friar understood that he was the cause of this torment, he slowed his work. He became so conscientious in his efforts to stay in line that he actually dropped several times behind it, and received as a reward several strokes of the long-lashed whip. The last of them, given with a certain drawing motion, cut his skin like a knife, and he felt the warm running of his blood as soon as the numbness of pain left his flesh.

He was not angered. It always seemed to Brother Pascual that the more pain we endure on earth, the nearer we have climbed to heaven. It was a doctrine which he would not preach to the simple mountaineers among whom he worked, because he felt that, after all, they have pain enough and need not be tormented by strange doctrines.

So he worked patiently through the day, with such a gentle and uncomplaining manner, that even the foul-faced criminals on either side of him began to look on him almost with kindness.

He was marched with the rest towards the sleep-house, at the close of the day. There all were taken through a certain ceremony.

In the first place—since uncleanliness may breed disease—they were driven like sheep through a river pool which soused them to the neck. After that they filed by a pile of tin cups, and past a big cauldron filled with a sort of bean soup, thick, sour to the nose, unspeakable to the palate, and on top of the cup of beans was dropped a lump of black bread.

This small ration they had only a short time to eat, because the guards grew restless and wished to have the end of the day come at once. Accordingly, the whips began to snap before the last mouthful was down, and then the doors of the sleep-house were opened.

Strange things happened then. For Brother Pascual saw men bolt out of the line and scream that they would die then and there sooner than spend one more night in the hell-house.

One ardent example put an end to this nonsense. The guards lassoed the first man to bolt from line, threw him flat on his face, and beat his back raw with their whips. Afterwards they threw him inside the threshold, since he was not able to walk, and over that prone body the rest of the condemned stumbled.

Once inside, each man made for a bunk, in a desperate

scramble. These bunks rose in tiers of five deep, with narrow aisles between them. The swiftest or the strongest took the lowest bunks, not because they were simply easier to reach, but because during the night the foul stench of humanity kept rising in the air. But many who lagged too far behind in the general rush got no place whatever for the night. And most of those who failed were the men who had been in the valley so long that the labour, the climate, the frightful food, had worn them to a frail shell.

They would die soon.

The big friar had managed to get himself into a bunk when he saw one of these staggering and haggard slaves go past him with a gesture of despair. The other labourers had found their places or were wandering like this lost one. So Brother Pascual stood down from his bunk. He picked up that miserable rack of bones and stretched the man in his place. There was not even strength in the man to sit up in speaking his thanks. He lay flat. His bony chest worked with short breathing; his belly, beneath the ribs, clung to his backbone. And as he muttered his thanks, his blue-coloured eyelids were already fast shut over his eyes. He looked to the friar like a man already dead.

"Brother," said the friar, his rumbling voice shaken with pity, "what is your name and why are you here?"

"Pedro Gonzales—Vera Cruz—robbery," muttered the voice.

"Robbery?"

"The butcher shop. I was drunk. Pulque. I saw the sausages and broke the window to get them."

"And they sent you here?" said the friar.

"I shall go very soon," said Pedro Gonzales. "Yesterday I fell to my knees once. To-day I fell twice.

Very soon they'll take the chains off. When a man cannot walk, then he's turned loose. And we crawl to the end of the valley. Some say that outside the pass there are men waiting with sweet water and pulque. Barrels of it. They have roast kid turning on the spits—tortillas——"

His mouth opened; he began to pant more audibly.

There was little light to see him by—only two lamps hanging from the ceiling in the whole of the big room—but what the friar could see of Pedro Gonzales made him drop to his knees.

He was still praying when a bull-toned voice bellowed through the room: "Who says that a friar is here? Who says that a big man, a giant, a priest or a friar, is here with us?"

The friar leaped from his prayer to his feet.

"Mateo!" he cried.

He heard a grunting answer, and then the thumping of heavy footfalls. Towards that sound he hurried in turn. And suddenly the tremendous grasp of Mateo Rubriz was on him. He put his huge arms around the bandit and crushed him with an embrace. It was like hugging a huge, rounded barrel.

"How have they brought you here? The dog Estrada—was it he? Answer me, brother—Mateo—my friend——"

"I came with El Keed, to find you, Mateo."

"*Madre mia!* To find—me? Here? You came willingly? Willingly do you say, Pascual?"

"Ay, willingly."

"And El Keed—he is here? Where is he?"

"In the hands of Juan-Silva."

"San Juan of Capistrano, forget all my prayers. Remember only this last one—let the hands of El Keed close on the windpipe of the devil, Juan-Silva! . . . Oh,

ascual, you have both come for me? But were you
mad?"

"It was the wit of El Keed. As for me, there is no
matter. But he thought if we came as though willingly
—we thought we might be made guards, and not
prisoners. Therefore we hoped that the time would
come when we could deliver you, Mateo, my brother."

Rubriz began to beat his breast with his great hands.
He began to weep, and the sound of his sobbing filled
all the room.

"What have I done that God should be so good to
me?" he said. He recovered his voice a little and went
on: "But I told you—I have always told you, Pascual—
that the saints had marked me out for a great thing.
Otherwise, why should they have given me two such
friends as you and El Keed. You—you are a man
living in goodness. But he is a gringo, a warrior, a wild
man who smiles at more things than we know. And
even El Keed has walked into hell for my sake?"

"He has come here. I told him to go back. I told
him that it was my duty, but his folly to come. And he
always said only, 'I have a friend——'"

Mateo cried out as though in pain.

"Now I am ready to die!" he said. "If only I could
kill Estrada with my hands and my teeth, then I would
be ready to die. What are the riches of Juan-Silva?
I have two friends! Pascual, I am ready to sing."

"It would be better to pray, brother," said the friar.
"Pray for El Keed!"

"I *shall* pray," said Mateo Rubriz. "And yet I have
a better hope than prayer. For the three of us—what
fools they were to let the three of us come into this one
valley! We shall find things to do. Do you doubt that?"

"I know that the mind of El Keed is never quiet. It
stirs even at night. I have heard him call out softly in

his sleep. Sometimes of horses, sometimes of guns, o
of gaming, or the name of a gringo girl or Rosita!"

"May a curse——" began Rubriz.

"Peace, brother," commanded the friar, with a certai
austerity. "She repents. And it is she who keeps th
good horses and waits for us outside the valley."

CHAPTER XXXI

MONTANA had come to strange hands and strange circumstances, and all was to him almost like a dream.

He had been taken, blood-dripping, naked, straight to the presence of terrible old Juan-Silva, and the ancient man had sat up and looked at the Kid with his eyes which were too young, saying: "It *is* El Keed! And now it shows that it is better to try a thing three times, so as to make perfectly sure. Did you get the right three, Emilio? That big Garcias with his murdering hands? And Leon? And that other, that Vidal? Did you get them all three—just those men? So much the better—three—and the time was how long? Twelve minutes do I hear you say? Then of course it is a proof that this is El Keed, and that El Keed knows how to see in the dark. And now it is time for us to treat our guest in another manner. Take him quickly, Emilio. You know where the rooms are where we give honour to a guest. Take him there. Open the press to him and let him find his clothes. Quickly! Quickly! So that he may change his mind about us!"

They took the Kid off in haste, therefore, and the grey-headed captain of the guard said, muttering:

"No man ever before was treated like this! Not even the tax-collectors! No one was ever treated like this. Some one is going mad. Some one is growing too old!"

There was everything that a man could wish, it seemed to the Kid, in the rooms to which he was taken. The ceilings were high. The air was heavenly cool, forced by fans through constantly showering water, the very sound of which ran like a blessing through the mind of Montana.

In the two rooms there were few pieces of furniture. The space, the coolness, the purity of the air were enough in the Valley of the Dead. On the floor were pieces of grass matting, woven in oddly pleasant designs. The chairs were wide, low, of native carved woods after very ancient patterns. And for a bath he stood in a rock-cut bowl that was sunk in the floor of a small room, while a pair of negroes poured buckets of tepid water over him. After that he saw what manner of clothes were provided by Juan-Silva for his guests in the Valley of the Dead. They might have suited some Arab chieftain —loose trousers of the thinnest and finest cotton, and a cloak of the same material that flowed over the shoulders, together with thin-soled sandals that had two cloth laces across the instep.

When he had dressed himself in this manner he was cool to the point of real comfort; and the pressure of hot blood was still gradually receding in his brain.

Juan-Silva sent for him. He went out and sat with the old man under the screen of feather-work, but the sun was slanting from the west, now, with less than half of its former strength. A Mexican woman brought them food. She looked like an ape, with a flat face stuck out at the end of a forward-leaning neck. She had a hump behind her shoulders that indicated strength rather than age, and her arms were prodigiously long. She brought them frothing chocolate, sweet cakes, and a snowy mountain of white sliced chicken meat to be eaten with hot peppers and tortillas.

Juan-Silva laid hold of her arm and stopped her.

"This is Maria," said Juan-Silva. "For ten years, now, she has been serving me. There was never a woman more faithful. Never one who worked for a master so patiently. And yet she is not paid with money."

Afterwards, while they were eating, the Kid said:
"Does she love you so much, señor?"

Juan-Silva parted his lips from his long teeth and laughed.

"You are not the first who came here of your free will. Maria came in the same way ten years ago. She had found out that her two sons had been sent here not many months before. But one of them was already dead, and the other she met crawling down the road. The chains had been taken from him. He was free!"

Juan-Silva interrupted himself to laugh again.

"So she had the pleasure of sitting down in the road and holding his head while he died. Afterwards, instead of putting her with the other women to work in the fields, I let her come into my house. Because I saw a thing in her eyes that was different. There was a light in her glance; there was something that went through me as fire shines through glass. I felt that she would not wear out soon. And so she is still here—and she is only waiting. She is paid by expectation."

"Waiting for what?" asked the Kid.

"For my death!" said Juan-Silva.

He rubbed his hands together and the sound was like the chafing of two pieces of paper.

"Since she watched her boy die and heard him curse me, she is certain in her soul that at the last moment I cannot die an ordinary death. The ground will open—devils will come out of hell and carry me away!"

He held his cup of chocolate in both his skinny claws and supped up the liquid noisily.

"She doesn't know, my friend—no one knows, except a few whom I have told, like you. But I shall not stay here in the Valley of the Dead until my life ends. All of this—all of these years—they are spent for a purpose."

There came over the Kid a curiosity which was greater than any torment of thirst.

"What purpose, señor?" he asked.

"Shall I open my heart to you?" croaked Juan-Silva. "Shall I tell you that I am barely forty thousand pesos from my goal? And then I may leave the Valley of the Dead—I may sail over the sea—I may go again to Old Spain!"

He made a pause, here, considering his thought before he went on:

"Thought is a living thing, my son, and desire must have words for its issuance. So I tell you because I like to sit here with you, and because I know that you—what you say—you are El Keed. Men have feared you and men have feared me. Therefore you will understand what I have to say."

Here he continued:

"When I was a boy I was a shepherd in old Castile. The land of castles! You understand what I say? A shepherd. That means to eat bread and drink water, wear one garment for five years, wrap up the feet in old pieces of leather, burn in summer, freeze in winter. People make the shepherds sing songs; but all that I heard from my companions was cursing. But always there was something above us!"

He pointed upward. Heaven? wondered the Kid.

The old man continued:

"There was always the castle on its rock. The trail wound up to it. The road was cut into the solid rock, and the castle stood on top. I climbed up and looked over the walls. I saw the courts inside. I saw the broken casements and the walls leaning. That was all that was left of the castle. In the old days there had been a reason for shepherds. They were the slaves of a master. They followed him to war, to be brained or lanced or stabbed in the battle by the iron-clad knights. But the castle was empty, and still we were all serfs. And as I walked with my sheep I used to look up and up, and I saw the castle and told myself that I would one day come to have a million pesos, and then I would buy that castle. Mind you, the greatest sum I could think of was a million. I placed it that high. I would have so much. I swore to my soul that I would become as rich as that. And I have never forgotten.

"Where is the fool and the scoundrel, *amigo*, except the man who contents himself with less than his soul desires? At last I saw that I must travel to a new world to find my fortune. I came to Mexico. I discovered this place where not money, but a strong heart and an iron will, were needed to make gold come out of the ground. And here I have remained ever since. You think, my friend, that these years in the Valley of the Dead have been a torment, but I tell you from my heart that every day since the beginning has been sweetened by the thought of the time to come. In the hot summer day I think of the castle holding its head among the blowing clouds. And in the winter I think of how my hall will be in Spain, and the great fire of logs burning on the hearth, and the light shining from the windows to tell every shuddering shepherd through the hills that Juan-Silva was once like them, and that now he is strong and rich and warm!"

He actually extended his hands before him and rubbed them together as though at this moment a winter chill struck through him with the memory.

And Montana wondered over him, vaguely, dimly. There was no other human being in the world with a heart so hard and with a soul so evil as that of Juan-Silva.

A consuming passion of interest arose in Montana to such a point that he no longer hated the old man. He wanted to read him for hours and weeks, as in a book one may find weird adventures.

He said, bluntly, "Will you have long with your castle?"

"Ah," grinned Juan-Silva, "you look at the body and you see that it is like old leather, ready to crack apart with a little bending. But the place to look is in the eyes of a man. Men have lived twenty years past a hundred. Considering them, I still have a third of my years to spend, and they shall be spent in my Spain, in my valley, in my castle on the rock. My relations will remember me, then, and they will come every year. They will come in flocks, offering me presents, waiting on me, each fighting to do more and more for the poor old man who is about to die. But the soul will not pass out of my body, *amigo,* until I have made them wait thirty or forty years. The fools that begin pampering me as boys will be grey-headed men before at last I die and they carry my body to the chapel where it will be wrapped in lead and lowered into a deep grave in holy ground. There I shall sleep sound, sound!"

He began to laugh once more. Even in his death he was to cheat the world.

"Poor Maria!" said Juan-Silva. "You see how she slaves for me? She is sure that in a year or two I shall die and she will be present to see my soul carried into hell. But as a matter of fact, she cannot tell that I am not far from my goal. A million pesos. Perhaps next year— perhaps the year after—the profits dwindle in this tobacco business, and there is always fresh money to be spent on the damned workers. These young men of to-day, they are worth nothing, *amigo.* Nothing, nothing! There was a time when I could take any youth in his twenties and rub him against the rib rocks of hell for ten years before his knees buckled under him and he fell. But nowadays all is changed. Some go mad in a week; some take fevers and die in a month. A lucky fellow am I to have a man last out three years of my service. There is no longer the old strength, the old endurance, and that is why my money builds slowly, slowly, slowly!"

He spoke with much bitterness.

"Ah, but that poor Maria!" chuckled the old man. "I have thought of one thing that I may be able to do for her—I may be able to take her down to the sea with me. I may bring her as far as Vera Cruz, and there she may stand on the wharf and watch the great ship sail, the ship that is taking me away from the Valley of the Dead and the ghosts of her sons, and carrying me softly and safely across the cool blue ocean, to my Spain and my castle. Hark to me, El Keed—when I think of that I can hear her screaming in my ear. Like music!"

CHAPTER XXXII

In the strange company of Juan-Silva the days might have gone swiftly enough for the Kid, but behind his mind there was the constant anxiety about Rubriz, about the friar.

When he felt that he had gained some foothold in the thought of the old man, he spoke to him one day when they were in Juan-Silva's carriage.

The carriage was his one great pride and extravagance. For it he kept constantly in his stable four fine horses, white as snow, and perfectly matched in size. On the driver's seat appeared a coachman. A footman was at his side, to spring down and open the very low-cut door when the master chose to dismount. And as the four white horses, at trot or canter, swept up the dusty road through the middle of the valley, drawing behind them the heavy, gilded extravagance of this vehicle, it was plain that Juan-Silva was allowing himself one foretaste of the glory that was to be his in his castle in Spain. And as they whirled along, now and again Juan-Silva would turn his head on his scrawny neck and look at the white dust that boiled up into a choking, hanging cloud behind him.

He took the Kid with him every day for a drive of inspection; and at last Montana said:

"Señor, there are two friends of mine in the valley. Be kind, and let me see them."

"The friar?" said Juan-Silva.

"He's one."

"My lad, think of the good he is doing! Think of the comfort that he spreads around him in the sleep-house! You would not want to take him away from those unlucky men!"

He gave his hoarse, croaking laugh.

And the Kid, looking down at his gripped hands, fiercely restrained the impulse to throttle the old fiend at once.

"But then, you have a second friend, El Keed?"

"Rubriz."

"Ha! Rubriz! But ask me for something I can give! The friar is a jewel to the other poor devils, and Rubriz is a jewel to me! What a man that is, my son! I have stopped the carriage and watched him leading the line of the workers. What a man! What a giant! Not tall, but vast. Vast as thought. An idea to fill even a strong brain! Mateo Rubriz—here in my valley—the great bandit—and now working, adding peso to peso for the sake of old Juan-Silva! Consider, in a sense, my obligation to Mexico!"

"Well," said the Kid, slowly, "I don't ask you to set him free. I ask to see him, only."

"To see him? To talk with him, you mean?"

"Yes."

"Ah, my son," said Juan-Silva, "why do you make me say no to you so often when I have nothing in my heart but a sense of kindness and even of gratitude to you because of our talks together and because of those old Spanish songs which you sing to me in the evening. Furthermore, I have in my mind a great purpose which perhaps you will bring about quickly. But as for letting you speak with the friar and Rubriz, consider, El Keed, that I know what you can do, in part. I have closed you with three strong men in a dark room. Strong men, desperate men, able to fight for their lives, fiercer than wolves in winter. And yet in a few moments they are dead. They are hacked to pieces. And El Keed walks out, unharmed. Now, then, suppose that I unite you even for a moment with two such as the good friar and that great Mateo Rubriz—how can I tell what miracle will happen then? This much I know—that not while I live will a man escape alive from the valley. But perhaps—three men together are a great strength!—perhaps you and your friends might work the miracle. They might pass the guard at the gate of the valley. They might pass even beyond the reach of those."

Here he paused, and pointed towards the wall of the valley. Along that wall three Indians were trotting their ponies. They rode with high stirrups, their bodies bowed over, their elbows flapping. And over each man's shoulder extended the long, shadowy line of a spear, ending in a head like a tuft of fine flame. They looked clumsy, unwieldy, but the Kid knew that, once roused to action, man and horse would become as one savage beast to pursue an enemy.

And behind that trio the dust rose from the hoofs of another set of three, and behind them still another appeared. Thinking of them, it seemed to the Kid that the strength of Juan-Silva extended even to the dim and distant line of the horizon. There was no escape. Night would never be thick enough to let men get so far from the valley that the winged hawks, the Indians, would not overtake them.

"Tell me, señor," said the Kid, "how you keep those Indians happy?"

"It is not hard," answered the old man. "Now and then some fool manages to escape from the sleep-house. He climbs the wall of the valley. Perhaps because of the darkness he gets away for a few miles into the hills. And the next morning the word goes out to my good red men. They sail out over the earth as buzzards sail out over the sky. They course here and there, and at last they always find the renegade, and they run him down, gradually; they help him forward with the tips of their lances. At last he falls on his face. Then four of them, perhaps, will run their spears through him and so bring him back to the valley and let the other workers see what has happened. And one Indian—he is their chief—runs his lance through the fallen man up to the butt, and so carries him back alone. And this is the beautiful part of that picture—that the man is young and strong and all of the life has not run out of him, so that he can still scream a little and still struggle with his hands and his feet. It is a very good sight, and there are no more attempts to escape from the valley for a long time!"

The Kid closed his eyes. He could see that "beautiful" picture too clearly. And he began to think, not for the first time, of Rosita, far out there in the hills—but not far enough, because she would keep herself always close enough to one high point so that she could see what was happening in the Valley of the Dead. Or had she given up her watch before this? Had she retired towards the land of the living?

She might find enough of the sun-starved grasses to serve as fodder for the horses, but how did her own food last? Or what traps had she contrived for the lean jack rabbits, since she dared not shoot for fear the noise might reach some distant ear?

He had lost his count of days. But time was like a hand pulling at him constantly, and the tenseness grew little by little until he knew that a breaking-point was near.

How he could help his friends—that was the chiefest of the miracles now. But he could see no step of his way towards it. He spent hours, in addition, wondering anxiously what that "great good" might be which Juan-Silva expected to draw from him. And then he learned.

He had gone to his room for the siesta hour after midday, and hardly had the cool showering noise of the water put him asleep before he was wakened by a knocking.

Old Maria stood inside his door.

"The master—Juan-Silver—he wants you," she said.

She remained there, standing back to let him pass through the door, and as he went by her she spoke:

"Your hands are free. Why don't you use them? Why do you wait to die like a poor blind sheep?"

He could not answer this. He walked on before her into the patio of Juan-Silva, and as he stepped out into the blinding strength of the sun he saw the carriage and the four white horses already harnessed and waiting, though it was hardly time for the master to begin his daily drive. There were sweat stains on the four, more-over, and a servant was now rubbing down the spokes of the wheels.

When he spoke to the mozo who held the heads of the leaders, the man said, with a grin:

"Great people have come—generals and great people!"

Old Maria still showed the way until she had opened the door into the main room of the house. It had the grace of a fountain set into the middle of the floor; and the light came from above through a skylight of thin, translucent slabs of green quartz.

The Kid, as he entered, was gripped by guards who waited on either side of the doorway. Then he saw before him the cause. For in the middle of the room, at a table with Juan-Silva, were the lean, yellow-green face of Jack Lascar, peak-faced Major Alvarez, and above all the swinish jowls of General Ignacio Estrada.

All heads turned towards him as he stood there, made helpless by the hands that were fastened on his arms.

And Juan-Silva said:

"Well, take your hands away from him. Even a great man like El Keed needs weapons. With his bare fists he can't do very much!"

CHAPTER XXXIII

So the Kid, made free, walked slowly on towards the table. Behind him, the guards were retiring from the room. Only old Maria remained to serve the guests, who already had before them little glasses of that fine, green-tasting fire, tequila.

It seemed to the Kid that he was advancing into an ethereal region, an atmosphere of pure hate. They were all smiling at him—Lascar, and the governor, and the major, and Juan-Silva.

The "great good" which Juan-Silva expected from him would be, no doubt, apparent on this day.

Jack Lascar rose from his place and bowed to him stiffly.

"Your pleasure, Montana," he said, "ain't half as great as mine."

"You're sitting in at a big game, Jack," answered Montana. "If you've got the cards, d'you think that you've got the stakes?"

"We're three with one thought, partner," said Lascar. "That thought is about you!"

"Sit down, my son," said Juan-Silva.

The Kid took a place at the end of the table, and old Maria, wooden-faced but with flame in her eye, poured out a glass of tequila for him.

"You, my general," said the old man, "should be the first one to speak."

At this, Estrada put out his hand flat on the table, the palm turned up, in the attitude of one who is about to make a great offer.

He said: "We should have met before. El Keed and Estrada have things to talk about. And, to be quick and short, Rubriz was carrying away from a place we know about, one-half of a thing which we both had seen."

As he said this, he put his other hand, in an unconscious gesture, over his heart.

"Now then," said the general, "what Rubriz was taking was restored—to a man who better knew how to use it. What I want to talk to you about is the second half! You can tell me where it is!"

"Not yet!" exclaimed Juan-Silva. "Not a word more to him, my son. I've named my price and I expect my money."

The general turned on him with a snarl.

"I could let in the light of a public examination on this hell-hole of yours!" he roared.

"Try, my general," said Juan-Silva. "Castilian brains are still the best, and Castilian money has been spent in the high places, friend!"

He began his cackling, husky laughter.

"Twenty thousand—twenty thousand, and every penny of it back unless he talks. Twenty thousand is a fortune, Juan-Silva."

"Thirty thousand," insisted Juan-Silva. "Thirty thousand, and not a peso less. Why, *amigo*, you might as well offer me twenty pesos as twenty thousand. Thirty is what I need and what I must have. It rounds out—it completes everything—it makes *me* a free man!"

"Free?" exclaimed Major Alvarez. "You mean that you'd leave the valley, then?"

"Ay, free to leave the valley—my purpose finished—the rest of my life to live—where I please!"

A queer, choking, bubbling sound came from the

throat of Maria. She covered her face with her hands and turned the noise into a coughing fit, but Montana saw that she was purple and swollen with some great and sudden emotion.

"Besides," said Juan-Silva, "I sent word to you about the sum I wanted before you could speak with El Keed. You have it with you?"

The general glared at him, his moustaches spreading and closing like the whiskers of a walrus.

Still with his glance of hate fixed on the old man, Estrada said:

"You have the money, Alvarez, and you have another part, Lascar. Put it on the table."

Each of them picked up from the floor very heavy bags. When they were dropped on the table the heavy wood was shaken by the impact.

"Let me see it—let me have a taste of it!" exclaimed Juan-Silva.

The mouths of the bags were, accordingly, untied, and as Alvarez pushed the top of the bag towards Juan-Silva a quantity of gold coin spilled out on to the table. One or two of the pieces rolled rapidly away. The ancient claws of Juan-Silva reached out and caught them. Then he leaned back in his chair, gasping for breath that had been crushed out of him by the high pressure of excitement.

"It is here—it is true!" said Juan-Silva. "It need not be counted. I trust you, gentlemen. I trust you perfectly. Maria—old fool—witch—tie up the bags again. Thirty thousand pesos! Thirty thousand——"

"And every coin of it back," said the general, "unless El Keed talks to us!"

"Ah, but he'll talk," said Juan-Silva.

He drifted his eyes over Montana and his cracking, parchment lips furled slowly back from his long teeth.

He shook his head, and the stiff fold of skin wobbled under his chin.

"El Keed has seen my little ways in the valley. He knows that I could persuade him to talk!"

"Do you think so?" said Montana, deliberately. He pointed at the other three. "You think, Juan-Silva, that I'll talk to them and tell them what I know about the other half of the emerald crown? Juan-Silva, you think that I'll talk and let them take me away, afterwards, to make sure that what I've told them is the truth?"

"There are ways of persuading you," said Juan-Silva, coldly.

"Try words, Juan-Silva," exclaimed the general. "I've tried persuading on Rubriz. I tried it until his body was bursting and dying with the persuasion I gave him. And still the beast would not speak a word. And this is another like Rubriz—or more so. Try persuasion before you try threats."

The old man held out his two hands.

"You," he said, "are children. Perhaps there is no other person in the world who understands how to move the minds of men—and their tongues—as I do. But—we try the soft way first. Shall I talk with him?"

"Alone," said the Kid. "I could make an agreement with you—but alone, Juan-Silva."

"Be careful of him," broke in the general. "This sort of a gringo devil, if he's cornered, would have the pleasure of killing you before he was killed himself. But listen to me—El Keed, listen. If you tell us where to find what we want, and if you come with us, by the sacred word of a Mexican gentleman, by the honour of an officer, you will not be harmed, and after we have found what we want, you go free. I swear all this!"

"Honour? Gentleman?" echoed the Kid, softly.

He looked neither at the general nor at Luis Alvarez, but stared at Jack Lascar, and a quick, twitching smile flared back the lips of Lascar, a wolf's grin. It was there for only a moment, and then it was gone, but from it Montana could see a clear picture of what his treatment would eventually be in the hands of the three.

He turned to Juan-Silva.

"I'll talk alone with you before I make up my mind," he said.

"Remember, Juan-Silva——" began Estrada.

But the old man held up his hands and smiled at them.

"Go into the other room. Show them the way, Maria. Give them drinks. My friend, El Keed, will talk with me alone. Perhaps we shall persuade one another to something worth while."

The general, nervous, glancing over his shoulder, left the room, shaking his head as he went. Maria passed in with them and closed the door, her tray of drinks shivering with a musical tinkling.

"Now?" said Juan-Silva, waiting.

"If I go with them," said Montana, "I go to my death. I want a price for that, just as you want a price for my talking."

"What price do you ask?" inquired the old man.

"Rubriz and Brother Pascual."

Juan-Silva smiled.

"El Keed is a good friend," said he. "And if they are set free—if they are sent out of the Valley of the Dead—what will men say of me?"

"You are leaving, yourself," answered Montana. "You have the money there that rounds out your fortune."

"True," said the old man; "but the valley remains as the source and the back log of my fortune. It must always be cared for tenderly—by me while I'm here, and by my lieutenants after me. But if Rubriz and the friar are set free—then you talk?"

"After that I can say a few more words to you—and perhaps then I can talk with Estrada. I can tell him exactly where to find the thing he wants."

"Good," murmured Juan-Silva.

Maria had come into the room.

"Call Emilio," said Juan-Silva.

She brought a guard instantly to the farther door.

"Get Rubriz and the friar," commanded Juan-Silva. "Knock off their chains and their steel collars, and bring them here."

The guard opened his eyes, backed through the doorway, and was gone.

After that, for a long moment, Juan-Silva fingered the fat sides of the bags of gold. In his bright eyes there was more life than ever.

"Tequila," he commanded Maria.

She filled his glass; and he sat for long minutes, sipping it. Now and then he lifted his glance to the Kid and smiled at him.

"What gratitude I feel to you," he said. "But I told you that I expected out of you a great good. And now, you see, the thing is here before me."

He touched the heavy bags with the tips of his fingers and began to daydream happily again.

After this long pause there was a tapping at a door, and a guard appeared to announce:

"They are put in the next room, señor. Both of them are there."

"They are there? And that is your payment, friend. Now, what do you ask me further than this, before you are paid in full, as I am paid—and I am free, El Keed, to leave the curse of the Valley of the Dead behind me— I am free for my valley in Spain where men forget the past because the present bites too hard and near the bone!"

Maria jerked her body straight, so that even the hump behind her shoulders disappeared for a moment, and the lines of her wooden face seemed to be stretching.

The Kid stood up from the table.

"I've heard that they're in the next room. Let me see them first, to make sure. Then I'll tell you the rest, Juan-Silva——"

He had turned his back while he was still speaking, when he heard behind him a rushing and a flopping noise, like the beating of wings, and a little rattling like the sound of dice in a box.

He whirled to see Maria with her hands fastened in the throat of old Juan-Silva. He was vainly beating at her face, tearing at her wrists with his claws, while as she shook him the teeth rattled together in his gaping mouth. Her ten years of waiting were not to be in vain; and if she could not see the very devils rise out of hell to take Juan-Silva, she would bring him death before he went on to freedom and a happy day.

The Kid ran for the struggling pair, but before he reached the spot, Maria had jumped back and run from the room, leaving the old man with his head fallen on his neck and a bloody froth on his lips.

He was not dead. But more than the blood on his mouth was the dimness of those unconquerable old eyes. Now, with a great struggle he brought his head erect. But he could not speak aloud. He could only whisper:

"The doctors! Save me, El Keed. Save me for the castle on the hill—the logs on the hearth—the lights in the windows——"

He crumpled, small as the body of a child, his head resting across his arms on the table.

The Kid was certain that this was death, but as he leaned over the body he heard a last faint whisper:

"And the damned shepherds freeze their feet in the frost outside——"

The last thought of Juan-Silva was, in his grim way, a happy one. Then a shudder shook him through his entire body. He began to slip sidewise in his chair, and when the Kid straightened the body again, the head fell loosely on the back of the chair, and dead, dim eyes looked up at Montana with an abstracted amusement.

CHAPTER XXXIV

ESTRADA, Jack Lascar, Luis Alvarez—these were small dangers—they were as nothing, now that the cruel brain of Juan-Silva was blank for ever. But the machine of Juan-Silva remained intact and strong. His Indians still rode the rounds of the valley; his guards were at the pass.

And then the Kid thought of two things—the carriage which waited in the patio with the four steaming white horses, and that singular gesture of Estrada towards his heart when he spoke of the lost emeralds of Our Lady of Guadalupe.

Whatever happened, he had more than his single pair of hands to work with, now. He was instantly at the door in the corner, and, wrenching it open, he looked in on Brother Pascual and Mateo Rubriz. They leaped up at the sight of him.

"I knew!" cried the friar. "I told Mateo that it was your work. I knew——"

"Peace, peace, Pascual!" exclaimed Rubriz, and he raised his hand to command silence, and waited for the words of the Kid.

" Juan-Silva sits dead in the next room—a woman was the finish of him," said the Kid. "In the room beyond that sits the general, Estrada, and Lascar and Major Alvarez beside him."

"God," murmured Rubriz, "has consented to fill my hands! I shall die happy, to-day! Where are they, *amigo?*"

There was this singular effect of long torment visible in Rubriz—his entire body, but above all his face, had lost flesh and grown refined. He seemed less gross, younger by years. And this transport of murderous enthusiasm gave an almost saintly glow to his features.

"Follow me," said Montana. "If I have half the wits of a child, I know that the second half of the crown of emeralds is under the coat of Estrada, near his heart. We must have it before we leave. Do you hear me, Mateo? Wipe the killing out of your mind. Think man!"

"Estrada only!" groaned Rubriz through his set teeth. "Let the others live, but give me Estrada. I can feel his life now. I can feel the heat of his throat under my fingers. I have dreamed of it every night, and that dream was sent from heaven!"

"Keep him back, Pascual," said the Kid—"he's turned into a wild beast—and I'll go forward with this myself, alone."

"No!" exclaimed Rubriz; "I shall be as a child in your hands, *amigo*. Do as you wish. Give commands and I obey them!"

"It is a day marked in heaven. We shall not fail," said the friar.

They entered again that big room where the fountain continued to toss up its whisper of spray; but the master of the house lay dead in his chair, staring at the ceiling.

"I am opening the door yonder," said Montana. "I shall ask Estrada to come in, alone. Stand one of you on each side of the door. Mind, the others must hear nothing, neither Alvarez nor Jack Lascar. But as Estrada comes through, make him speechless. See that he has no chance even to kick his feet against the floor.

First help me to arrange Juan-Silva so that he seems living. So!"

They worked with him, silently, as he wiped the red from the lips of the dead man and drew him back in his chair so that his head was at a balance, supported against the high back of the chair. His lower jaw they could not keep from sagging, so that he seemed to be continually grinning at some inward jest.

"Now," said Montana, and he strode on past the fountain, to the door of that farther room out of which the voice of great-throated Estrada was making a steady rumbling.

One glance the Kid gave to either side, and saw that Rubriz and the huge friar were each in place.

Then he thrust the door open, and saw the general walking back and forth, with a stream of tobacco smoke blowing over his shoulders from his cigar. The major and Jack Lascar were sprawling in chairs out of which they leaped at the sight of the Kid.

He smiled back at them, a very slow smile of a genuine amusement.

"Juan-Silva wants to speak to you now," he said.

"Come, Lascar," said the general. "Come with me, Alvarez."

"Only General Estrada," said the Kid. "Juan-Silva wants to talk to the general alone—or with me present."

"Go out there with that death's-head and you—alone?" said Estrada. "Does he think that I'm mad?"

"Well," said the Kid, "if you won't talk to him alone, it seems that you won't talk to him at all. Shall I tell him that?"

The general looked rather wildly about him.

"Stay here!" urged Lascar through the twisting side of his mouth. "Never anything better than bullets came out of the Kid."

"Go, for God's sake!" said Major Alvarez. "Or are we to stay for ever in this hell-hole?"

The general took the cigar from his mouth, looked down in doubt at the mangled end of it, clapped it back into his face, and with a frown of military courage strode straight for the door as one resolved.

"The general is coming," called the Kid, over his shoulder, and as Estrada crossed the threshold he quickly closed the door behind him.

Turning, he heard a soft beating in the air. That was all. The vast arms of Brother Pascual had made Estrada helpless at the first grip. And the grasp of Rubriz silenced him, so that the general gaped his mouth wider than his moustache was long, and thrust out the red of his tongue.

So they bore the general into the middle of the room.

By that time his two guns were in the hands of Montana, and the weight of the revolvers seemed to clothe the Kid with a new strength.

Perhaps it was mere chance that made the friar deposit Estrada in the chair opposite to the death grin of Juan-Silva. But the sight of that hideous grimace turned the governor rigid. His throat had been so bruised by the fingers of Rubriz that he was groaning a little with each breath that he drew; but that was an involuntary sound.

He offered no resistance as the Kid tore his uniform coat open and reached inside it. There, in a soft coating of chamois, he felt the hardness of metal, and knew that his guess had been right. He gave one glance inside the leather and saw the green of the emeralds. That was enough. He flashed the gold and the green at Rubriz and then dropped it into his pocket.

Brother Pascual and the outlaw, in the meantime, had bound the general to the chair he sat in.

"This Lascar," said the Kid, leaning over the gaping face of Estrada. "How did you manage to find him?"

But the general, between sight of the dead man and fear for his own life, could not speak. He could only stare upwards with empty eyes. However, the mystery could not be very profound. The hate of Lascar would have taken him as far as Duraya along the trail of Montana; and there most naturally he would have been introduced by that very hatred to Estrada.

"Now!" Rubriz was whispering; "now he cannot be heard even to fall—and he must die, Montana!"

"Kill a helpless man?" answered the Kid. "I'd rather eat bad meat—and so would you. Mateo, we have only seconds. You hear me? Only seconds to start. That pair won't wait for ever in the next room. The guards may break in at any moment. Will you listen to me?"

Mateo Rubriz, standing back from the bound and gagged general, folded his arms and they rose almost to his chin with the greatness of the breath he drew. But then, gradually relaxing, he was heard to mutter:

"San Juan of Capistrano, keep my hands from him. Save this dog meat for the dogs!"

"Now, Mateo—now, Pascual—we have the other pair. Here we have guns. And there are only two. You first, Mateo. The sight of you will cool their blood for them, and we'll have them in ropes before they've got over their chill."

Mateo looked at his friend sidewise, with a grin wider than that of a snarling cat. Then he went to the door, with Montana at his heels, and threw it open. The long-stepping Pascual was right behind them.

They went over the threshold with their guns before them, walking gingerly, as men must do unless they wish to disturb their aim.

There was not a word spoken. Lascar, when he saw them coming, sprang up from the table and let a cigar fall from his mouth. A bubbling scream got half-way up the throat of Alvarez and stuck there. Then the two put their hands above their heads. To ask for mercy was a folly. They said nothing as the cords were fastened about their wrists. Then Pascual took them out of the room to the table where the dead man and the living prisoner already waited.

They were bound into chairs, before Mateo, stepping back, drew a forefinger significantly through the air.

"So?" he said. "So, *amigo*, and they are dead; they bubble a little of their own blood in their throats—and that is the end."

"No!" answered Montana.

Rubriz stared at him.

"There is this little softness in you, like a girl," he declared. "Otherwise, what a man you would be, my friend!"

"If we cut their throats," said the Kid, "it would be less credit to your San Juan of Capistrano. See what he has done for us!"

"Ah hai!" exclaimed Rubriz. "And who will say that he is not the best saint in the world, now?"

"Search them, first—search every inch of them," said the Kid.

They searched, quickly, using the flat of the hand carefully to feel whatever lay in pockets. And that was how Pascual suddenly produced from Alvarez the gleaming green eye of the last emerald.

He held it up. To him it was a lasting miracle, a thing to fill the soul. But Rubriz and Montana were of a more mundane mind. They did not even heed the agonized rolling of the eyes of the gagged Alvarez, as though his heart itself had been plucked from him.

The Kid was already speaking.

"We have one passport, and only one. That's the word of Juan-Silva. He'll never write again, and the best we can do is to take him with us. Pascual, wrap that scarf on the chair—wrap it around his skinny neck and see if that will keep his mouth closed."

The friar obeyed. This nearness to death kept him murmuring—perhaps unconsciously—swift words of prayer. And as he twisted the scarf's length strongly around the neck of Juan-Silva, the pressure of the upper layers of the cloth forced the jaws to close. Only a faint sardonic smile remained on the face of the old man. And when the Kid, with a touch, opened the eyes wider, a perfect look of naturalness took the place of the death gape.

"I am going out into the patio, there, to be the coachman," said Montana. "There's no weight to Juan-Silva. You can seem to be merely walking beside him, and you can hold him up. Pascual—draw that end of the scarf down his back under his cloak. Now if you keep a hand on that, his head will be raised. Not too much. He always walked with it bent forward. Support him— one of you on each side. I'll back the carriage to the door. When you hear the wheels, open the door and come straight out with the dead man between you—quickly, too, so that the swing of his legs may look like walking. I'll try to keep the eye of the people yonder. One chance in ten, brothers—our only chance!"

CHAPTER XXXV

At the door, the Kid turned and looked back. Already the two had lifted Juan-Silva from his chair. They walked across the floor, but it was a sad imitation of the walking of a living being. The trailing legs swayed back, pitching the top of the body forward a little, and the head, though held up by the scarf, was pulled too much to one side.

A black pang of desperation struck through the brain of Montana. But he gathered himself for half a second, and then stepped out into the white blaze of the patio. There was a pair of guards on the farther side of the open space, in the shadow of the wall. They were smoking their cigarettes, idly. And the heads of the leaders were held, now, by a mere house mozo.

The Kid sprang up lightly into the driver's place and gathered the reins, singing out:

"Let their heads go, boy!"

One of the guards, calmly, deliberately, raised his rifle to his shoulder.

"El Keed!" he called out. "Get down from that place!"

The Kid merely tossed him a phrase across his shoulder.

"Why do you think Juan-Silva has been taking me out with him every day? Because he wants a real coachman, *amigo*."

With that he swung the leaders, and backed the wheelers with a strong pull. The carriage lurched well back to the main door of the house from which he had just stepped.

"Why should I not?" he heard one guard saying; and the other: "Put down your gun, you fool! I have seen Juan-Silva making him a friend. Look! Here's the señor himself!"

With his heart in his throat, choking him, the Kid snapped the whip and cut the near leader so that the horse reared straight up, striking at the air as the powerful wrench on the reins kept him from lunging forward. He seemed almost as though he might topple backwards, for an instant, and in that instant the Kid felt the carriage sag and sway beneath him.

"The friar and Rubriz—Mateo Rubriz! By God, I won't believe my eyes!" one guard was saying, jerking up his rifle uncertainly.

"Be still, you fool! See, they are arm in arm with Juan-Silva!"

And, risking one glance behind him, Montana saw that the dead man sat well back upon the cushion of the rear seat, between the burly forms of Rubriz and the friar.

He swung the leaders at the same time towards the archway that opened from the patio to the valley road, and as he did so he saw the servant who had been holding the heads of the leaders standing agape with great eyes of horror.

That man had seen too much. In another moment his voice might begin to speak words that would bring all the men of the household lurching in pursuit—but, ah, to be through the shadow of that arch and into the open road!

He controlled the leaders to a mere prancing walk, nevertheless, as they went under the black of the shadow.

"Good day, señor!" sang out a guard, saluting.

There was no answer. There never would be any answer.

But now the team was in the road. The carriage swayed on to the crest of the shallow grade, and the Kid gladly let those four fine animals strike hard against their collars.

"Don't look back till we come to the bend of the road!" called the Kid, without turning his head. "Then see what's happening behind us, for God's sake!"

At a smart clipping trot he sent the team forward, and as they took the bend of the road towards the lower valley he heard Rubriz cry out, exultantly:

"There's nothing! We're clear of them!"

"Look again!" called the Kid, "but don't crane your neck. And keep Juan-Silva straight in his place."

"The barelegged mozo has run out into the road," said Rubriz. "He's pointing after us. The two guards are out there with him. Put the whip on the horses! Make them gallop—for our lives, Montana!"

"No; they may be only suspecting. They'll hardly be knowing—not yet!" said the Kid. "Is there an alarm signal in the valley?"

Still at a brisk trot, he drove the team towards the lower mouth of the Valley of the Dead. And he heard Rubriz make answer:

"Three shots—a time between each one. That's the alarm. I've heard it fired only once—and that time they brought the runaway back dead! But they won't bring us. Now the whip, the whip, Montana!"

"Steady, steady!" answered the Kid, never turning his head. "There's the guard at the mouth of the valley. Have you forgotten them? Do you think we can ride them down, Mateo? Keep the dead body straight. Look to the face of it. Don't let the mouth sag. You hear?"

"I hear—and God forgive me!" exclaimed Brother Pascual.

They were far down the valley, now, and before them the narrow pass opened like a pair of sharp jaws. Out of the shadows of the rocks swarmed the ten or a dozen guards on their active mustangs, and the heart of the Kid fell a little when he saw among them the grey head of that same captain who had commanded here on the day when he and Pascual had walked so serenely past the lips of hell and into the hot throat of it.

He saw the lean, naked arm of the man rise in a signal—the other horsemen instantly spread to each side of the road.

Then, high-pealing, he heard the challenge:

"Halt, there!"

The Kid stood up in his place.

"You goat-faced, chicken-legged baboon!" he shouted, keeping the horses at the full trot, "are you stopping the señor himself?"

The grey-head jerked himself high in his stirrups under the impact of those insults, but the name of the "señor" had the effect of checking and bewildering him.

How close they were, now, to at least the outer fringe and margin of freedom!

But here the captain shouted loudly:

"Rubriz—the friar—*madre mia!*—Rubriz! Take aim, everyone. Halt, El Keed! Halt or we shoot the horses first and you second."

Halt? And let the captain, then, have a chance to ask Juan-Silva a question that could not be answered by those dead lips?

The Kid looked wildly back, and he saw the two friends seated dauntlessly erect and—between them, the frail body of Juan-Silva, and the jolting of the carriage made his head jar up and down a little, as though nodding in animated conversation to which Rubriz, towards whom the dead head was turned, seemed to be making quick responses. Ah! God bless the cold nerve and the ready wit of Mateo! And both he and the friar, with the hands which were nearest to the dead man, were supporting him beneath the light folds of his cotton cloak.

That nodding head, and the now partly opened mouth of the dead man—might they not seem like life if no pause were made?

He had seen these things at a glance, and instantly he was calling to the grey captain: "Ask the señor himself, you mule's head! By God! You'll be back with a hoe and in chains before this day is ended! Out of my path! Away with you!"

And with the long lash of his whip, leaning forward, he slashed the horse of a rider who was trying to push in ahead of the team.

"For the last time!" yelled the grey captain. "Halt, for your life! El Keed, halt!"

"Señor Juan-Silva!" cried the Kid. "Do you hear him? Do you hear the drunken fool?"

"It is Rubriz! By the Mother of Heaven, it *is* Rubriz! Where are you taking him?"

"Where Juan-Silva wants him to be. Eat that and choke on it!" cried the Kid.

"On your own head!" yelled the captain. "Fire!"

And then, his voice pitched as high as a scream, almost, he cried out the counter-command.

"Hold your fire! Hold your fire! My God! my brain's turning—but—the señor——"

And jerking his cantering horse to a halt, he saluted with all dignity while the carriage sped past him, and instantly was out of view around the next bend of the pass.

"Oh, my brother," groaned the voice of the friar, "even the blessed saints have no more wit and no more courage!"

They swung out into the open, and there lay the empty road stretching endlessly before them towards a horizon that could never be reached, it seemed. And at the very instant of passing the teeth of danger, it seemed to the Kid that they had accomplished nothing— that all remained to be done.

He heard a gunshot, then. And looking up to the left, he saw a trio of Indians riding in the distance at full speed. One of them had fired the first shot, and at an interval another gun exploded. And still a few counts later, a third was fired, the heavy report floating slowly down to them. It was the alarm, and now the Valley of the Dead would do its best to recover its lost ones.

CHAPTER XXXVI

THERE was no more trotting, now. Rubriz and the friar pitched the body of Juan-Silva headlong from the carriage. The frail form of the dead man struck the ground, rolled thrice over, and lay still, grinning face upturned to that bitter sun which for these many years had tortured so many unfortunates in the Valley of the Dead. He, at least, could look at it with unwinking eyes, as at a friend.

And the Kid, lashing the horses to a running gallop, felt the carriage leaping and bucking behind him.

"The guard is through the gate of the valley," shouted Rubriz. "They are riding hard, but they're far away. And the damned Indians have rough ground to cover before they'll ever get down to us. Can we cut the horses out of the harness and ride away like that? Now, *amigo*, while there's still time!"

"Pascual can hardly ride a mule. Do you think he could keep his place bareback on one of these white devils?"

"True!" said Rubriz, groaning.

"Take the horses and away with you!" called the friar. "Take them, brothers. Why do you throw yourselves away for me? Montana—Mateo—my friends —farewell!"

The Kid looked back and saw the good friar in the act of leaping from the carriage which his weight encumbered. But Rubriz grappled with the big man and dragged him back.

"Stay with us, Pascual!" cried the Kid. "If you

leave us, we have to stop and fight for you. Pray for us, Pascual!"

The friar was too simple to see through this device, and dropping instantly on his knees, since he needed the grip of one hand to keep himself from being jounced out of the carriage, he raised the other in what might be called half of the gesture of supplication, exclaiming in his tremendous voice:

"Almighty Father, breathe the breath of lightness into the bodies of these good horses. Give them strength and give them courage. Make the sand deep and soft as mud beneath the hoofs of those who follow us!"

And the four white horses proved worthy of their breeding and their price, now, racing with equal strides, their ears flattened. It would not be an easy race, no matter who won. But now the wrenching, tugging, unequal weight of the carriage began to tell. As it swerved through the ruts, over the shelving surface of that half-made road, more than once it threw a wheeler out of stride. And the reins and the whip of the Kid were busy constantly picking up this horse and steadying that.

He drove well, though that was not his special art. But when he looked back he saw that the men of the valley were gaining, undoubtedly, and still faster the Indians who rushed on a dozen ponies over the higher ground on the left were pulling up. Already they were almost abreast. A little more and they would be able to shoot down from the hillside and cut off the retreat.

It was the eye of Rubriz that saw the promise of help, and the voice of Rubriz that shouted like ten trumpets.

"Do you see, Montana? It is your red mare—it is my black horse—and that is Rosita Santos. Rosita, divine, beautiful, blessed! I strike the lips that spat at

249

you. I beat my head in the dust before you. Child—angel—glorious Rosita, for your sake I love, I cherish, I worship all women!"

It was she, beyond all doubt, looking small as a boy, and riding like a trained jockey as she shot on her own fine mustang out of a gap between the hills and headed for them with the red mare and the black stallion sweeping along beside her.

Blind men could have known what her purpose was, and the Indians and the men of the valley were far from blind. The thin, distant sounds of their yelling blew like small horns into the ear of Montana.

Here were three horses, to be sure. But four were needed. Well, as for the mule of the friar, it could never have kept pace. And one of the white horses of the team had to be used.

Who could do it? Not the girl. And red Sally could be ridden, as yet, by none saving himself. And then that problem was solved by Mateo Rubriz. He swung on to the driver's seat. He leaped far out from it, landed on the back of the near wheeler, spilled almost off from it, and then righted himself and rode erect. He waved his hand behind him, laughing up like a happy child at the Kid.

"It is I, Rubriz!" he shouted. "I have him! It is my part. Only the black will carry the bones of Pascual. When you stop for Rosita—God bless her!—help me only one instant to cut this fellow loose."

The girl was nearing them, now. The wind of her riding struck her like a current of water, clove to her. And she reached out her right hand, shouting. Every sound of her voice struck through the heart of the Kid like a mighty chord sung by a thousand sweet voices.

"The black horse for you, Pascual!" he called over his shoulder. "Steady all. I throw on the brake!"

It screeched, the wooden blocks grinding on the iron tyres as the Kid checked the rush of the horses with all his might. And then down into the tangle. He caught the knife from the hand of the girl and slashed. The leather traces were shorn, the long reins gashed in two, and in a moment Mateo Rubriz, on the bare back of the white wheeler, was galloping straight ahead down the road. For he knew that the girl's mustang, the red mare, and the black horse were all fresh, but the white was tired, very tired, already, and with no feather's weight on its back.

They raced their horses for distance.

And then they were running for time, with a sun that sloped with a maddening slowness towards the western horizon. For the pursuit could not gain and the weary white horse held back the four fugitives. More than once, bullets sang in the air, but the distance was entirely too great; only a random shot could strike them. At last the Kid brought Sally close beside the white. He took the hand of Rubriz and lifted twenty pounds, thirty pounds, forty pounds of the bulk of the big rider, transferring it thus to the strong back and the tireless, iron legs of red Sally. There was no faltering in her, and it was her strength that carried them into the red of the sunset, and suddenly into the quick twilight that securely covered them from further pursuit at that moment.

All pursuit was not ended, of course, unless those savage riders from the Valley of the Dead gave a little more thought to their memory of Juan-Silva, smiling open-eyed at the sun. But the truth was that they had neither sight nor sound of an enemy all the way to Duraya.

But the taste of life was so exceedingly sweet to them all, after the Valley of the Dead, that the precious trinket inside the bit of chamois was never unwrapped once during the entire journey. Perhaps there never was a happier journey, in spite of the sand-filled winds that whipped and choked them, and the foul water, and the starvation rations most of the way, and the reason for that happiness was that here were four who had been through fire together, so that they knew the temper of one another. And what is happiness in this world?

The Kid described it well enough. They had come into the green of living mountains—living with grass and with trees and with water after the naked desert they had crossed. The Kid himself as the evening closed in, had brought down with two shots from one of Estrada's revolvers a deer that leaped out before them from a thicket. But it was not the good, hearty stomach-filling meal nor the sweeter smoke that followed it that made the Kid speak. He said, into the dark of the night, to the three faces about him that he had come to love, all softly stained by the firelight:

"Being happy—that's being rich. Being rich is not money. But it's owning not miles of land, either. But owning people. Not slaves. But people you own, and they own you, and you can walk farther into the heart of a friend than a sailor can sail a ship on the sea."

This was so obvious to them all that no one made a comment. They sat silent, looking at one another, watching the firelight die and then glancing up at the stars in heaven. They sat there so long that Brother Pascual finally went to sleep with his back to a tree and forgot to say his evening prayer; but when he remembered this omission the next day, he could not find it a weight on his tender conscience.

Rosita stood leaning against a tree, just then, tapping with her slender fingers against the rough of the bark.

"Tell me, Mateo," she said, "if you have forgiven this gringo? Have you forgiven him, and forgotten?"

"I?" exclaimed Rubriz—but even he guarded his voice so that it might not enter the sleep and disturb the dreams of Pascual. "If I forgive him, may San Juan of Capistrano never forgive me or be aiding me again! What? A man-stealer who caught away Tonio from me? Forgive him? I'll see him damned before I forgive him."

He half raised himself and glared at Montana, who lay flat on his back now, with his hands cupped at the back of his head.

"Ay, Mateo," said the Kid dreamily, "I've always known it. Some day I'll have my thumbs in the soft of your throat and break your windpipe between them."

Rubriz made a sound as though he were drawing water, not air, through his set teeth.

"But when you are dead," said Rubriz, "San Juan strike me if I shall not be a little sad."

"Well," said Montana, in his gentle voice, "when I've buried you, I'll get a thick-headed bulldog and call him Rubriz, and that will take your place well enough."

"Ah-h-h!" murmured Rubriz, coming softly, catlike, to his knees and one hand.

"Be still, Mateo!" commanded the girl.

"You would help him, eh?" demanded Rubriz. "And yet God knows how many of your countrymen he has butchered like sheep."

She went to Montana and leaned over him.

"What am I to you, devil of a gringo?" she asked.

"Sit down here and I'll tell you," said Montana.

She sat down at once, and he moved until his head rested in her lap.

"Now tell me," said the girl.

"Afterwards," said he, "I'll tell you how much I love you, but now I wish to sleep. Sing to me, Rosita."

"Ah," said the girl, "tell me if I hate you or love you most!"

"Sing to me," insisted Montana, "and you'll find the answer in the songs."

She laughed a little, and then she began to sing in a voice smaller than speech. Rubriz strained his ears to catch the sounds. He could see the dimness of her hands smoothing the brow of the Kid.

When they came into Duraya, in the middle of the night, they climbed, all four, to the room of the bishop.

He rose from prayer to greet them. He was very tired, very weary. But when he saw them a strength flowed suddenly back through him.

"My children," he said, "are you the ones who went to the Valley of the Dead and undid the work of the devil there? Was it you who turned the slaves loose?"

"Loose?" exclaimed Rubriz. "Do you mean to say that the slaves broke loose?"

"We only have rumours and whispers," said the bishop. "I know nothing for certain except that the soldiers are rushing towards the Valley of the Dead and extending long cordons to sweep up the escaped men. And inside the valley, Juan-Silva and the general himself were found dead and terribly mangled, and that Alvarez and another man were killed, also, together with a great many of the guards. It is a dreadful thing—and it happened, I hear, while most of the guards were rushing away to try to recapture daring prisoners who were escaping in the carriage of Juan-Silva himself! Ah, El

Keed! Do I see you holding the reins? But I have been kneeling here in prayer for Juan-Silva!"

"All the saints praying would never be any good to the soul of Juan-Silva," said Rubriz.

"Perhaps not," said the bishop, "but I like hard tasks. What is this, brother?"

For Pascual, patiently, was holding up the broken half of the emerald crown in one hand, and the lost jewel of Alvarez lay in the other palm. The bishop took up the treasure as though it were truly composed of green fire. He raised it in his joined hands high above his head.

One could forget, then, his meagre nightgown, his bare feet with the wind blowing on his shanks. Perhaps it was unclerical for a bishop to be seen in this informal garb by a woman, but since he had one arm, at that time, about the shoulders of Rosita, the bishop did not seem to be troubled.

"Well," said Rubriz, "the devil had no commission for this job, except that most of the work was done by a gringo."

"Hush!" said the bishop. "Who can speak of the devil where there has been the manifest hand of God?"

He went on talking to Rubriz, for a time, and to big Pascual, who was smiling like a child, his two great hands clasped together.

And at last Bishop Emiliano said:

"But I have not said a word of thanks to my son Montana. Where has he gone? And where is Rosita?"

"El Keed," said Rubriz, "why should he care about thanks when he has Rosita?"

And all three of them, on a sudden impulse, leaned out of the window and looked down. There in the thick gloom of the street they could see a man and a woman walking slowly, their heads bowed close together.

"Hai!" said Rubriz. "Can't he find women in his own country? Does the gringo dog come down here to steal our girls away from us?"

"And our hearts, brother," said Pascual.

"Ay," grunted Rubriz, "these gringos they stop at nothing—they will have all."